THE FAE BOUND

RITE WORLD 8: RITE OF THE WOLF

JULIANA HAYGERT

COPYRIGHT

This book is a work of fiction. Names, characters, places, and incidents either are products of the author's imagination or are used fictitiously. Any resemblance to actual persons, living or dead, events, or locales is entirely coincidental.

Manufactured in the United States of America.

First Edition July 2020

www.JulianaHaygert.com

Cover design by Moonchildljilja

❀ Created with Vellum

AUTHOR'S NOTE

I hope you enjoy reading *The Fae Bound*!

Don't forget to sign up for my Newsletter to find out about new releases, cover reveals, giveaways, and more!

If you want to see exclusive teasers, help me decide on covers, read excerpts, talk about books, etc, join my reader group on Facebook: Juliana's Club!

RITE WORLD

Welcome to the RITE WORLD!

Free Novella:
The Vampire Hunt

Rite World:
The Vampire Heir (Book 1)
The Witch Queen (Book 2)
The Immortal Vow (Book 3)
The Warlock Lord (Book 4)
The Wolf Consort (Book 5)
The Crystal Rose (Book 6)
The Wolf Forsaken (Book 7)
The Fae Bound (Book 8)
The Blood Pact (Book 9)

Rite World: Blackthorn Hunters Academy
The Demons Kiss (Book 1)

The Hunter Secret (Book 2)
The Soul Bond (Book 3)
The Shadow Trials (Book 4)
The Immortal Vow (Book 5)

And more to come!

THE VAMPIRE HUNT

I have an exclusive novella set in the Rite World that is just for my newsletter subscribers!

Click here to sign-up and receive your book!

THE VAMPIRE HUNT
A Rite World Novella

Norah is a demon hunter, one of the best graduated from the Blackthorn Hunters Academy. When she's sent to investigate a case concerning demons in a small town, she runs into a very arrogant vampire. Her first instinct is to kill him, after all, he's a supernatural and demon hunters are taught to end all evil.

Cain is a vampire prince. Because of his status, he's in charge of making sure humans don't find out about his kind. During a routine investigation, he bumps into a very sexy demon hunter and he wonders what she's doing on his way.

However, the case grows much bigger for Norah and Cain to handle alone. To find the truth and win this battle, the vampire and the demon hunter will have to hunt together —without killing each other.

How well could this end?

1

THIS WAS SUPPOSED TO BE A PARTY, SO WHY I FELT ANYTHING but happy?

Seated at the throne that suddenly appeared beside Lark's at the main hall of the Shade Fortress after our wedding, I watched as the reception raged on. Even though it had been sudden, Lark had found a way to throw a huge party, complete with performers and fireworks.

The fae, all from the shadow court, indulged in the food and drink and dance, most already too drunk to even remember their name. Amid them all, Lark talked to other male fae. He laughed out loud and patted their backs, sometimes moving his arms wide, as if he too was drunk, but I knew better. He had been holding the same damn glass of champagne since the beginning of the party hours ago, and he had barely drunk a single sip so far. He was pretending to be drunk, though I had to admit he did look happy.

The complete opposite of me.

Every now and then, his dark eyes met mine from across the room, and it was all I could do not to flinch in disgust. But I kept it in. I held on his stare with a defiance of my own. Yes, I had married the fae prince, but that didn't mean I had to like it.

In fact, I despised it.

During the entire party, no one approached me. No one came to talk to me, except for a few servants who offered me food and drink. Still feeling sick about my unknown future, I refused those.

While the fae danced and chatted and drunk, I stayed seated and quiet on the throne, staring at the wall across the room, above everyone's heads, and counting the seconds.

Finally, when the sun was rising behind the mountain, Lark dropped his champagne flute and walked to me. By now, there only a handful of fae still dancing on the main hall, while most of them had already left, or slept on the floor, too drunk to care.

With an easy smile, Lark halted before me. "Ready to go?"

My stomach twisted in a million knots. No, I wanted to answer him. But I knew better than to tell him that. So when he offered me his arm, I stood from the throne chair and took it. Like a gentleman, he helped down the dais steps, then guided me over the black carpet cutting through the main hall. Outside, his guards waited. Once we walked by them, they counted five steps, then began following us.

I wasn't overly worried about the wedding night,

because it was different for the fae. We had a rule called the Moon Period. The fae couldn't sleep together for three weeks after a wedding to seal the magical bond between them and wait for the mating bond to snap before trying to conceive a child, since creating a baby fae wasn't as easy as it was for humans.

Lark confirmed as much when he stopped in front of the closed doors to my chambers, his guards several steps back now.

The prince held both my hands this time. "I never thought much about the Moon Period until now." He stared into my eyes, the glint in his downright naughty. "But I understand its importance. I want to have many sons with you, Farrah, and I'll respect the Moon Period."

Two feelings warred inside me: relief that he wouldn't touch me tonight, but despair that soon the Moon Period would be over, and then I didn't know how I would keep him away from me.

What he didn't know, though, was that I couldn't give him any sons. Or daughters. Fae could only have children with those they had first been with, and for me that was Wyatt.

Wyatt was my mate and I hadn't even had the chance to tell him.

Even if I had the chance, would I have told him? There was no reason to make him more worried and sad about our situation. Not knowing he was my mate would help him move on faster.

Lark brought one of my hands to his lips and planted a kiss on my knuckles. "Sleep well, princess."

With a last lingering glance, he retreated. His guards followed, except for two, who positioned themselves on the hallways, a good way from my door.

Holding my chin high, I entered my chambers. But once I closed the door behind me, I broke down. Angry tears filled my eyes and I grabbed at the white dress, ripping it to pieces.

The tears slipped along with the pieces, scattering across the floor until I could barely see the smooth dark stone underneath. Only once I was free of that, I wiped my tears away and took a deep breath in.

No, I couldn't break down. Not now, not later. This was my life now and if I broke down now, what would happen to me for the rest of eternity? Because fae lived forever.

And Prince Lark was my husband forever now.

That knowledge, that fact, brought a sharp pain to my chest.

The idea of running away with the medallion fleeted through my mind, but I pushed away. Because running away wouldn't solve anything; it would only make things worse. But most of all, Lark wasn't an idiot. He had known I came to him using a medallion. He had taken it from me earlier.

But I had another thing he didn't know about it. I hurried to the closet, where earlier I had hidden the looking glass under some dresses, hoping no one would find it.

My hands shook as I held the looking glass.

I closed my eyes and willed it to work.

When I looked at it again, the glass had become a

canvas swirling with smoke. I held my breath as the smoke cleared and the image took shape.

It was me, sitting in an armchair, wearing a long, blue dress, with a big smile on my face. I opened my arms and someone, a little boy, ran to me. He jumped on my arms and hugged me tight. When he glanced up at me, I could see it. The boy could be young, but he had Wyatt's hair, Wyatt's eyes, Wyatt's smile.

I almost dropped the looking glass.

What did this mean?

Then, the image was gone and the looking glass returned to its normal form.

"What the hell," I muttered shaking it, as if that would make it work. Usually, the damn thing showed three scenes, not just one.

I put the looking glass back into its hiding place and dragged my feet to the window. The sun was rising, tinting the mountain with orange and yellow light. For a moment, I closed my eyes and let the sun's warmth kiss my skin. If only life was this easy and kind.

But it wasn't. I leaned over the window and glanced down. The fortress stretched under my window, with many turrets and sharp points, and beyond it, was the harsh mountain.

From here, no one could resist a fall, not even a fae.

But killing myself wasn't the answer to this problem. Running away wasn't either.

Then how could I make my cursed life a little easier to bear? Become a dutiful wife and bow my head to Prince Lark? Not in a million years.

There was only one more solution I could see, one I had no idea how I would accomplish, but ... I couldn't just pretend I was a pretty doll. I couldn't just sit here and accept my fate.

Somehow, before the Moon Period was over, I was going to kill the prince.

2

THIS COULDN'T BE HAPPENING.

Even though I was sure Farrah was already wed to Prince Lark, I had tried entering the fortress many times, but every time I was stopped either by a horde of shadow fae soldiers guarding every entrance of the fortress, or by Ariella, who told me I would be killing myself.

She was right, I knew that, but I couldn't just give up. Beyond these trees, beyond the walls of the fortress, was Farrah. So close. There had to be a way of saving her from him.

"She doesn't need saving," Ariella said more than once. "She chose this."

I knew that too, but I couldn't believe that. I knew what Farrah was doing. She was sacrificing herself for her people. That hardly seemed fair.

After many botched attempts to sneak into the fortress, I let Ariella guide me deeper into the forest, where we wouldn't be found out by the shadow fae patrolling the area. She was sure they were expecting me and searching for me, with every intention to kill on sight.

I paced around the fallen tree trunk Ariella was seated at, my mind racing, my emotions buzzing, my blood boiling.

"Wyatt, you have been like that for hours now," Ariella said, her voice hard. For an angel, she was quite the tough one. "You have to stop and rest and relax if you want to keep going later."

I stopped, but I didn't relax. I glared at her. "I don't want to keep going later. I want to keep going now."

Ariella rolled her eyes, annoyed at me. Yes, I had been in this fucking state for hours now, and honestly, I couldn't see myself relaxing until I was able to rescue Farrah from the Shade Fortress.

"I know you want to *save* Farrah, and if you're so adamant about it, we will, but we can't just charge into the fortress now. It'll never work. We need another angle."

Fuck, she was right. I knew that. But it was hard to admit it.

With a heavy sigh, I finally succumbed and plopped down on the tree trunk beside her, the full force of my failure hitting me square in my chest. Holy fuck, I had let Farrah slip through my fingers and now she was the prince's prisoner.

There had to be something—

I slipped my hand inside my jacket and found something. Frowning, I pulled the blue stone Spencer had given to me before opening the portal for me. I stared at it.

"Do you have any idea what this is?" I asked, showing the stone to Ariella.

She took it from me, lifted up to the sky, turned it around. "Nope." She shook her head and returned it to me. "Why? It's supposed to do something? I couldn't sense any magic coming from it."

I raised an eyebrow at her. "Can you sense magic?"

"It depends. I never could pinpoint how it works, but sometimes I can feel magic coming from a person or an object." She shrugged. "There must be a rule, I just don't know it yet."

"Interesting," I muttered. I turned the stone around my fingers. "Anyway, an old fae gave me this stone before I came back. He told me to give this to Farrah. That it was crucial."

Ariella frowned. "How did he know about Farrah?"

"I have no fucking idea." I tucked the stone back into my pocket. "But if he knew about Farrah and me just like that, this means he knows more stuff, right?" I wanted to believe Spencer had some kind of super sixth sense, and he could predict something would happen. Like me taking the stone to Farrah would somehow help me in rescuing her. Otherwise, the alternative, that he was just plain crazy and came up with crazy things, was too disappointing.

"I'm afraid this Spencer guy is in the fae realm, though," Ariella said. "We can't get to him now."

Fuck, that was true. "What can we do then?"

After a moment of silence, Ariella glanced at me, the wheels inside her mind visibly turning behind her blue eyes. "What do you know about Blaze fae?"

"Just that they are one of the four more powerful kinds of fae in the fae realm, why?"

"Because I've heard about them before. When I was looking for the demons who took my wings, I heard there was a large camp of Blaze fae near the Grand Canyon, that they had come to hide after a big war they had against the shadow fae."

"So?" I asked, impatient about her point.

"So, if we can convince them to start the war again, but on Earth this time, we'll have help to rescue Farrah."

I shot to my feet. "They would do the heavy lifting for us."

Ariella stood before me. "Right."

A sense of purpose filled me. The Grand Canyon was far away from here, but if we got allies to help us fight, it would be worth it. Though it pained me to leave Farrah with Prince Lark, I knew he wouldn't hurt her. She would be safe for a couple more days.

"All right, then, let's go to the Grand Canyon."

I started marching toward the nearest road. Ariella caught up with me in no time, and we discussed a quick plan on the way. Steal a car, drive to the Grand Canyon, search for the blaze fae. If we didn't find them right away, we would try to find someone who had heard about them. Then we would convince them to fight the shadow fae stationed in the human realm.

But, before we reached the road, a group of women dressed in black clothes stepped in our way.

"Hello there," one of them said, with a toothy smile. "I'm Myra from the Bonecrown Coven."

My body stiffened. The Bonecrown witches. The ones that had kidnapped Farrah to use her in a blood sacrifice, but instead beat her up and let her to die alone in the forest.

Why the fuck were they here?

3

FARRAH

IF I HAD TO MEASURE MY ETERNITY BY MY FIRST THREE DAYS in the Shade Fortress, I would say I was in for a boring life. During the day, Lark called on me to be by his side almost all day. First for breakfast, then for a walk in the courtyard in the center of the fortress, next for an audience with his people, where he sat at his throne and I sat in mine, and the shadow fae residing nearby came to tell their grievances to the prince. Most of the time, Lark seemed indifferent about the people's problems, but here and there he showed some emotion, especially when it was all about revenge.

Once, I became too curious and asked him why the hell there were shadow fae living in the human world. Didn't that mean they would also lose their powers, grow old, and die? Very happy with my sudden interest, Lark explained that his fortress was protected with his father's magic, which didn't allow anyone inside, plus the shadow fae residing nearby to suffer like the frost fae had.

After our boring morning, we had lunch. After lunch, Lark met with General Auron and his soldiers for a meeting—this one I wasn't invited to. Later in the evening, Lark called me again to watch him train with his soldiers in the training center underground, just above the dungeons. I couldn't deny he was an expert fighter and his magic was immense. If I had ever to face him, I knew without a doubt that he would win easily.

So I scratched "fighting the prince" off my list.

At night, after he showered, we had dinner, then we had another boring walk along the courtyard before Lark escorted me to my chambers, where I was supposed to stay until he came back for me the next day.

Besides the time when he listened to his people and *I* wanted to do more than he did, Lark's day was simple. Normal. Boring.

Still, my mind didn't stop working the entire day. How could I kill the fae prince if he was too strong for me, and he was always surrounded by his guards?

I only saw two solutions: I either killed him in his sleep by sneaking up in his chambers, pretending to want to be with him, or by poisoning.

What I needed was to research about poisons. Thank goodness, this damn fortress had a huge library. While Lark met up with his general and soldiers, I snuck into the library.

I made sure to pile my table with books about fae legends and some fiction stories, most about love and hope. If someone came to me, they would think I loved to read romance.

But, hidden underneath those, were books about herbs and alchemy. I had been searching for books about poisons, but I couldn't find any. Either Lark didn't have any, or they were somewhere else.

It was okay. Even if I didn't find anything specific, I was sure I could find about some lethal herb.

On my fourth day at the Shade Fortress, Lark's meeting lasted longer than usual, giving me more time alone at the library. Thankfully, he hadn't appointed guards to follow me around, like they followed him. It wasn't as if he needed them, not with some many guards spread around the hallways, and this damn fortress which was ... well, a fortress. It was impossible to get in, and it was just as hard to get out.

The library was endless and while perusing, I did see some fiction books that caught my attention. If I ever had some leisure time, I would pick them up to read them.

Alas, I didn't have any leisure time. Even if I didn't have what to do with my time, it would never be leisure. Not while I lived in this place.

With a sigh, I advanced toward another row of shelves. I had been exploring shelf by shelf, from top to bottom, and slowly covering the entire library. The books were divided into sections and topics, but sometimes I found a small area that seemed out of place. This would be so much easier if Lark had caught up with modern days and had a computer here with all the books in the library on a database.

I kept going, careful to read each one of the titles on

the bindings, making sure I didn't miss anything that could be useful.

After going through three long rows and finding nothing, I stopped and looked around. At this rate, it would take me a whole month to cover the entire library. I didn't have that time. In less than a month, the Moon Period would be over and I had to kill Lark before that.

This was ridiculous.

Trying to change my strategy a little bit, I went to the very end of the library. I would start over from here and then go row by row, until I met where I last stopped.

But it wasn't necessary. When I got to the end of the first row, I found a small section on magical potions and dark spells. Hopeful, I pulled out a handful of books and skimmed through them. Some had sections on poisons!

A sudden eagerness filled me. I could do this. I just had to find the right poison.

I sat down on the cold, dark stone floor and started browsing the books. It didn't take long. I finally found a poison that seemed strong enough to kill a powerful fae. But it took two weeks to brew and required three very rare ingredients: wolfsbane, darkmallow, and faerend.

These herbs could only be found in the fae realm, and I was stuck here, in this fortress in the human world.

I clutched the book tight to my chest.

Somehow, I had to find a way to get out and find these ingredients.

4

THE MUSCLES IN MY BODY TENSED AND I STARED DOWN THE three witches in front of us. Unfortunately, there was no way to measure how fucking powerful they were just by looking at them.

"What are you doing here?" I asked.

Myra cocked her head to the side. "Don't you know? I'm looking for the fae that escaped our clutches."

"I don't know what you're talking about," I lied. I knew exactly who she was talking about. When I first met Farrah, she had been in a trap left by the Bonecrown witches.

Myra took one step forward, her eyes gaining an amused glint. "I think you do."

Beside me, Ariella stole a glance at me.

"I thought ..." I frowned, trying to choose my words carefully. "Haven't your coven helped Luana and Keeran?" Over three years ago, the queen of the Bonecrown coven had welcomed Luana and Keeran into their estate and helped them learn about Keeran's past. "I thought you had turned a new leaf."

A smile stretched over Myra's red lips. "What, are you saying we're evil? We like to think of ourselves as neutral. We side with whoever has our best interest. In that case, we helped Luana and Keeran because it fit our own needs."

"And what's your excuse now?"

"Now, we have some unfinished business with Farrah." Myra's smile faded. "Where is she?"

"I don't know," I lied.

Myra narrowed her eyes. "You're lying. Where are you hiding her?"

I shrugged. "I'm not hiding her." That wasn't a lie at all.

Myra didn't like my answer. She raised her hand and a ray of black magic shot out, coming for me. I jumped out of the way and shifted into my werewolf form.

The three witches attacked full force, and Ariella and I fought back. Myra commanded the show, throwing black bolts at us while the other two witches followed her. I lunged into one, dropping her hard on the ground. I would have gone for her throat, but Myra shot a bolt at my side, making me skid away.

I growled at her.

Then Ariella stepped up her game. She invoked her magic, casting bright light all around us, just like she had done with the fae when she helped Farrah rescue me. The witches shrieked, covering their eyes.

I retreated, closer to Ariella. She purposely aimed her magic away from me, but I still couldn't open my eyes. She nudged my side with her foot, pushing me back. I kept retreating, but felt as her light became stronger, brighter, and the witches shrieked more.

After a moment, Ariella was by my side. "Run," she told me. "The light won't hold forever."

Relying on my senses, I ran beside her, away from the witches.

When it was safe, she let me know and I opened my eyes.

Then we ran some more.

***

Ariella and I were mostly in silence as we drove for three entire days, changing borrowed cars at least once a day.

When driving through Colorado, I couldn't contain my nervousness. I didn't like being back here.

"I see you're all jittery," Ariella said from behind the wheel. We had been taking turns driving every few hours, so we could rest. "Is it because of the witches?"

I shook my head. "No, I don't care about them." Even if they found Farrah inside the Shade Fortress, they had no way of getting to her.

"Then what's going on?"

I glanced out the window, to the mountain range rising beside the road, and let out a long sigh. "About two years ago, I've got in some trouble on this side of the country. I ended up pissing off some demons." That was putting it lightly, but I wouldn't bore her with my fucking story now. No one knew about it, other than me and the demons, and I sure hoped it stayed forever like that. "I just hope we don't run into them while we're around here."

Ariella tsked. "Well, too bad, because I'm looking to get some payback on demons, and I would gladly like to run into some."

I snorted. Of course she would. Demons had taken her wings, and because of that, she couldn't go back home, wherever that was. Well, if she ever found the demons who took her wings, I would help her catch and beat them up.

We fell into silence again until we reached a small town near the Grand Canyon. We sneaked into a group of tourists and joined them on a tour of the Grand Canyon. When they stopped by the Skywalk, Ariella and I sneaked out again.

I hiked the backpack I had prepared higher on my shoulders as Ariella and I started walking into more isolated areas, where no tourists should wander to.

"Do you know where we're going?" I asked Ariella after we had been trekking through the area for over two hours. Here, the sun was too hot, and the air dry for my lungs.

"I think so," she said. "I've heard they were hiding on this side of the canyon."

I frowned. That wasn't very helpful. Besides, whoever told her that could have been dreaming or drunk. I should have researched more about this before simply following her out here.

Another thirty minutes passed and the sun began setting. If we didn't find them soon, I—

"Here." Ariella stopped by a cliffside and pointed down.

I rushed to her side and looked down at the canyon.

And saw nothing.

"Here what?"

She glanced at me. "Oh, right, you probably can't see it. It's hidden with magic. But right down there—" she pointed her finger down again "—is a small town, and I believe the people living there are the blaze fae."

5

FARRAH

I PACED MY ROOM, MY MIND REELING.

It had been another day since I found out which poison I could brew to kill the fae prince, but so far, I had no idea how I was going to get the three herbs I needed.

My only idea so far was to sneak into the infirmary and the kitchen during the night, while most fae were probably sleeping, and try to steal it. I would have to worry only about avoiding guards stationed at strategic places and the patrols.

But it was still too risky. The chances of me actually making it to the infirmary or the kitchen without being caught were very, very low.

What other option did I have?

A soft knock came from my door and I didn't need to look up to know who it was. A small female fae entered the room with her head low, her shoulders hunched. She closed the door and approached me, her eyes on the floor.

"I'm here to help you get dressed for dinner, your high-ness," she said in a small voice.

I grunted. Since before the wedding, I had gained a servant of my own—a young wind fae who seemed to be scared of her own shadow. The fae only spoke to me about getting dressed, doing my hair, or retouching my makeup, nothing else.

I didn't want to sit through another dinner with Lark, pretending to enjoy his company, or at least, not mind it. A surge of anger and frustration rushed through me, but I kept it hidden. I couldn't lash out at this fae. It wasn't her fault I was in this situation.

I had made the damn deal with Lark. I had sealed my own doom.

With another grunt, I stepped into my closet, the young fae following me. She stopped behind me and started unbuttoning my dress. Though the many buttons would have been tricky, I felt unnecessary to have a servant help me get dressed and undressed. I could very well put on my own clothes, do my hair, and apply my makeup. But I stayed quiet and just let her do it since Lark put her up to it. I didn't want to anger him or draw more of his attention right now.

The dress fell to my feet. I stepped away from it.

The fae leaned forward and picked up. That was when I saw it—a purple bruise hiding on her back, near her shoulder blades, peeking from underneath her black uniform. I squinted, watching as she hung the dress on its place and started rummaging to find another. She lifted her arms, and her sleeve rode down a little, showing off another bruise, green this time, on her forearm.

What was going on here?

I opened my mouth to call her but realized I didn't know her name. "Hm, what's your name?"

The fae stilled, her hands froze over the dresses. "Hm, Jennie, your highness."

"Jennie," I said, taking her hands into mine and turning her to me. I lifted the sleeve of her uniform, revealing even more green and purple bruises. "What happened to you?"

She recoiled, stepping back and hiding her arms behind herself. She stared at the floor. "Nothing, your highness."

"These don't look like nothing." A feeling I couldn't explain took hold of me. "Jennie, look at me." The young fae kept staring down. "I don't want to order you to look at me. Please."

With a sniffle, the young fae finally rose her head and her eyes met mine. My heart squeezed at the sight of her unshed tears and the red bruise on her temple, and the small cut on the bridge of her nose.

"I-it's nothing, your highness," she insisted, her voice breaking.

This was ridiculous. "Who did this to you?" The fae returned her gaze to the floor. "Jennie, tell me who did this to you."

A sob ripped through her throat. "It was Prince Lark, your highness."

I clenched my fists and gritted my teeth. It was all I

could do not to go after him right now and accuse him of being worse than a monster.

"How did it happen?" I asked, my tone soft.

Jennie hesitated, but finally said, "My family and I lived in the fae realm. but we had a lot of debt. My father was caught gambling, trying to pay off the debts, but he just got drunk, buried us under more debt, and started a fight with a high ranking officer from the king's army." She wiped at the tears rolling down her cheeks. "My entire family was arrested. My father was executed and my mother, my sister, and I were sent here, to work as servants in the prince's fortress."

"Where are your mother and sister?"

"Dead," she said with another sob. "Prince Lark likes to gather the servants with criminal pasts and teach them a lesson." She gestured to her wounds. "Many of them don't survive."

My stomach curled at the thought. "That's absurd."

I hurt for Jennie, but her predicament gave me an idea. She looked young and naive, probably gullible. Maybe I could enlist her to help me find the ingredients for the poison ... though, I didn't trust being outright about it.

Instead, I plastered a fearful expression on my face. "I didn't know about this violent side of the prince. He's very eager to have a son, but ..." I rubbed my hand over my belly. "I'm afraid it will take a long time and he'll show his discontent about it by using his fists on me too."

Jennie's eyes widened, meeting mine again. "He wouldn't beat you up, your highness. He loves you."

I fought a grimace. I didn't think the sick bastard loved

me. I thought he was obsessed with me, in a twisted, sick way. "I don't want to risk it." Then I lowered my voice, as if this was a huge secret. "I've learned about a fertility potion that female fae should drink during the Moon Period, so they are ready to conceive when the time comes. However, I can't prepare this surprise for Lark if he sees me picking out herbs from the fortress' supplies." I paused, batting my eyelashes at her with a demure smile. "Would you help me? Would you get the ingredients for me?"

Jennie frowned, but then nodded. "If it means the prince will be happy with you and won't ever hurt you, I'll do it."

I sighed in relief. "Wonderful." I turned back into the bedroom and picked up the list I had hidden inside the nightstand's drawer. "These are the three ingredients I need." I offered the paper to Jennie. "But remember, this is a secret, a surprise for the prince. No one should see you gathering the herbs."

With a small grin of her own, Jennie picked up the paper. "I can do it." She folded the paper and slipped inside one of the pockets of her uniform.

I smiled at her, as if I had found my new best friend.

I felt bad for using her, but for some reason, I knew I could trust her with this. Finally, I was seeing a light at the end of the tunnel.

6

WYATT

IT DIDN'T TAKE LONG FOR THE BLAZE FAE TO REALIZE THEY weren't alone in the canyon. As Ariella and I approached their hidden town, which I still couldn't see, a handful of soldiers, all dressed in dark red uniform ran to us, pointing their spears at our chests.

"Who are you?" a male fae with long brown hair asked.

"I'm Wyatt, this is Ariella," I said, putting on my best business mien. "I'm here to talk to your leader."

The male fae frowned, considering. After a minute, he nodded once. "Follow me."

He turned and started walking deeper into the canyon. Ariella and I fell into step behind him, and the other soldiers flanked us. They lowered their spears, but kept them close and ready. We weren't prisoners, but we certainly weren't free to roam around here.

After a few steps, a jolt of energy coursed through me and the scenery before me changed. Now I could see the town: many side-by-side brown and reddish houses, nestled against the canyon, forming narrow roads that ran deep into the gorge.

Soldiers patrolled the street while blaze fae spied from their houses as we walked by one of the roads. We were escorted to what I thought was the center of the small town, where a bigger building stood in front of a large square.

"This way," the fae guiding us said, gesturing to the front doors of the building.

We stepped into a foyer that opened up to several doors. He took us through the one on the back, the largest one.

Inside was a meeting room with a long rectangle table and a high chair at one of the ends. A male fae with a few wrinkles and long red hair stood from this chair, followed by a young female fae on his right side.

They stared at us with inquisitive eyes.

"What's going on?" the red-haired fae asked.

The other fae lowered his head. "Lord Alos, this werewolf and this fallen angel asked to see you."

Beside me, Ariella seethed. From what Farrah had told me, Ariella was a fallen angel, but she didn't like to be called that.

Lord Alos narrowed his eyes at me. "Why have you come here?"

"Because I heard the blaze fae has a score to settle with the shadow fae," I said, going directly to the point. I had no reason to drag this on. "And I want to take them down."

Lord Alos stared at me for a moment, considering. "Why?"

I inhaled deeply and told them about Farrah. That she was a frost fae who was now locked inside the Shade Fortress, how her people had suffered in the hands of the shadow fae, and how the prince was just plain evil and had to be defeated.

"I know you want to take them down as much as I do," I continued. "I know Ariella and I are only two, but we're powerful. Together with your people, we might have a chance to infiltrate the Shade Fortress and defeat the prince. Once he's out of the picture, it'll destabilize the shadow fae, providing an opportunity for you to start a war, and this time, win."

Alos didn't seem convinced. "You seem to know a lot about fae and our history."

I puffed out my chest. "My mate is a frost fae. I made it my business to find out as much as I could about fae."

"What you're asking for ... it's tempting, but it's too risky," Lord Alos said. "I won't put my people at risk for a young female fae."

I knew it wouldn't be easy to convince him, but I didn't have many more arguments to offer.

"If you help us take down the prince," Ariella started, "we'll help you with your war. We'll stay with you until the end, and we'll make sure you win."

Lord Alos rubbed his chin.

The young female fae leaned closer to him and whispered something so low, even I couldn't hear it. She had the same red hair as Lord Alos, though hers was tied into a long braid.

Lord Alos nodded at her. "My daughter, Kayden, has an offer."

She turned to her, her amber eyes blazing. "We won't give you an army, but I'll join you in your quest. If we infiltrate the shadow fortress and kill the shadow prince, then we'll rage war against the rest of the shadow fae. And you will join us."

I clenched my teeth. Just one fucking blaze fae? Well, that was better than nothing, but probably not enough. "I'm assuming you're a good warrior."

Kayden's lips curled in a taunting grin.

Lord Alos snorted. "She's the best warrior the blaze fae has ever had. If she joins you, you're sure to win."

I glanced at Ariella. This was between the two of us. We came for an army, but we were being offered just one measly fae. Would that be enough? Would she still stand beside me and help me rescue Farrah?

As if reading my mind, Ariella gave me a sharp nod.

"All right," I said, a little irritated by the situation, but also relieved we didn't come this way for nothing. "We'll accept your offer."

***

AFTER OUR MEETING, ARIELLA AND I WERE ESCORTED TO A small house at the edge of town.

"You can spend the night here," Kayden said, opening the front door to us. "Someone will come with food later."

I frowned as I looked inside the simple house. "We're not allowed to leave the house?"

"You can," she said, calmly. "But we won't be responsible for your safety. After the war and being chased out of our own realm, the Blaze fae isn't very trusting, especially of other races. It's better if you stay in."

"We will," Ariella answered for both of us.

Kayden glanced at us. "We'll leave tomorrow morning before dawn." She turned and left, without waiting for a reply.

Ariella and I stepped into the house. I didn't even glance around and explore the place. I simply dragged my feet to one of the two bedrooms and plopped down on the bed.

Arms crossed, Ariella watched me from the door. "Taking a nap at this time of night?"

"No, not a nap," I mumbled. After so many fucking days driving like crazy and being worried out of my mind, my body was exhausted. I wanted to crash and slumber for a hundred years. "I'm turning in for the night."

"Oh, okay." She stepped out of the room and grabbed the doorknob. "Good night."

The door closed with a soft click, and I closed my eyes, willing sleep to come take me and shut down my many thoughts.

I fell asleep and dreamed of Farrah being held by Prince Lark, being in chains while he tortured her people in front of her. The prince laughed, saying it was all a trick. That he never intended to let her people out of the hook. That they would all suffer while she spent eternity with him.

I woke up with a gasp, sitting up in bed.

A second later, my senses became alert, but it was too late.

Hands clasped around my mouth and arms and legs.

I jerked, trying to get rid of them. I began shifting until something hard bumped into my head, and I fell into darkness.

7

FARRAH

It had been three days since I had first told Jennie that I needed the herbs for my potion. I got tense every second of the day, thinking she had told someone and prince Lark had heard about it. I was sure he wouldn't believe this fertility potion nonsense for a second and would know I was up to something. Each time he approached me with a sly grin, my heart stopped. But nothing happened. I felt like I was freaking out for nothing.

Though, it wasn't for nothing. Time was flying and soon I wouldn't have time to brew this damn poison before the Moon Period was over. I had to start it soon, or it would all be over.

Last night, I tried stealing the medallion off one of the guards, so I could go to the fae realm and get the herbs myself, but I was almost caught. All right, then that plan was out of question.

It was late at night and I was ready to lie down on my bed when Jennie slipped into my chambers.

"I've got it, your highness," she whispered, walking to me on her tiptoes.

"The herbs?" I asked, my voice just as low as hers. Here, no one could hear us, but one couldn't be too careful.

"No, I couldn't find those herbs anywhere in the fortress, but I got this." She lifted a medallion from the pocket of her uniform. "I borrowed it from one of the ladies in the court. I have to return it before morning, or she'll notice it's gone."

My heart beat wildly in my chest. It was not the herbs, but this was the next best thing. I caught the medallion from her and cradled it against my chest. "Thank you."

"I'll stay here and watch out for danger while you go to the fae realm and get your herbs," Jennie suggested.

I nodded, standing up from my bed. I rushed to my closet to change out of my nightgown—I couldn't go hunting for herbs in the fae realm in those—but stopped halfway when the doors to my chambers opened.

Prince Lark sauntered into the room and I quickly hid the medallion behind my back.

He didn't spare a single glance to Jennie as he said, "Leave us."

The young fae shot me a quick glance, but she was too afraid to confront him. Shaking from head to toes, Jennie bowed to him and scurried out of the chambers and closed the doors behind her.

Then it was just the prince and me and the medallion.

With what was supposed to be an endearing grin, Lark stalked to me. I slowly retreated, until my back hit the tall dresser along the wall. While he focused on my face, I hid the medallion behind one of the big vases over the dresser, hoping he wouldn't notice it.

Lark halted just one foot from me. "I'm sorry for coming so late. I just ... I needed to see you." He lifted his hand and ran his fingertips over my cheek. I tensed, suppressing the disgusted shudder that wanted to run through my body. "You're so beautiful, my dear Farrah. Waiting for the Moon Period to be over is *hard*."

He leaned into me, his mouth coming for mine, and I inhaled sharply, suddenly in panic mode. I tried enduring it, I told myself I could do, I could just kiss him. It wouldn't mean anything. But I couldn't.

On the last second, I turned my face. Lark exhaled, his nose rubbing my cheek.

"Sorry," I muttered. "I'm just not ready yet."

He pulled back and stared into my eyes. "You have a little over two weeks to be ready," he said, a new hard edge to his voice. He took a step back. "Good night, my dear Farrah."

"Good night," I whispered.

The prince whirled around and marched out of my chambers.

When the door closed behind him, my legs gave out and I leaned heavily over the dresser. I couldn't keep doing this. I could barely kiss him, I couldn't even consider the idea of sleeping with him. And once he found out I couldn't give him children, what would he do? Punish me? Torture me? Kill me?

A new idea came into my mind. If only I could steal a dagger or even a kitchen knife, I could slit his throat when the Moon Period was over and he finally came for me.

But that would certainly get me killed too, since his soldiers wouldn't just sit and watch as their prince died.

Regardless, if I failed to concoct the poison, that was my plan. Better to be killed than to live with this monster.

With renewed purpose, I grabbed the medallion from its hiding place and opened the portal to the fae realm. I stepped through, determined to find all the herbs I needed.

8

BEFORE I OPENED MY EYES, I FIRST NOTICED THE FUCKING ache on the back of my head. What the ...

Then I remembered what happened and shot up. And immediately was brought down by the shackles on my wrists and the long chains bolted to the walls.

"What the—" I swallowed my words as I realized not just my head hurt. I had bruises all over my body and all of my muscles hurt. Then a man walked toward me. No, not a man. A demon. "Drollmor," I muttered.

"Oh, so you at least remember my name." Drollmor was a high-level demon, one with enough power to look like a human all the time. Right now, he wore an olive skin and short, brown hair, with the sides neatly shaved. His face was angular and his body was big, as if he was a heavy weightlifter. "I've been looking all over for you."

I shook my head. Holy fuck, this couldn't be happening. "Fuck you," I said through gritted teeth.

"No, werewolf, fuck you." Drollmor tilted his head at

me. "You thought I wouldn't find you? That I wouldn't make you pay for our deal? You got what you wanted, now it's my turn."

I jerked against the chains. "You know I won't go down easy."

An amused grin spread over Drollmor's lips. "You're the one shackled in a building full of demons. I think you'll go down just fine."

He took a step toward me, and I stilled. My mind spun, searching for a plan, as I strained against the chains, using my werewolf strength to try to break them. But they barely budged. Fuck, what did I do know?

Drollmor brought his hands up, toward me.

"Master," a voice came from behind him.

Snarling, Drollmor turned around. He faced the demon standing on the wall on the other side of the room. "What?" he barked.

The demon lowered his head. "I just thought you would like to know, master, but the southpoint warehouse is being attacked by demon hunters."

A string of curses I didn't know crossed through Drollmor's lips.

There was one thing Drollmor hated more than the people who owed him a deal—demon hunters.

Drollmor brought his dark eyes to me again. "This isn't over."

Then he left, following the other demon out of the room. The door closed with a heavy thud and I heard the sound of several bolts clicking into place.

I didn't waste time.

I closed my eyes and focused, using my strength to pull at the chains. I braced my core and gritted my teeth. Pain laced my muscles at the struggle, but I didn't dare to give up. It was this pain, or having my soul taken to the underworld.

I would take the fucking pain any day.

Finally, I felt the chains budging. After another bout of struggle, they snapped from the walls.

I fell on my face, catching my breath and easing my muscles. But I still didn't have time to waste, I had to get out of here right now. Against the pain coursing through my body and the dizziness brought on my head blow, I pushed to my feet and stalked to the door.

I checked and yes, the door was locked. Again, I tapped into my strength and pushed against the door. It was even harder than snapping the chains, but after a while, I broke it down with a loud bang.

Fuck. If there were any demons left in this place, they had sure heard this. Even though I didn't know where I was and which direction I should go, I shifted into my werewolf form and bolted.

I made it out of a stone manor surrounded by woods and was momentarily blinded by the bright sun shining overhead. That was when I finally heard the shouts of Drollmor's lesser demons coming for me. As if I would stick around and wait for them to catch up with me.

I didn't slow down as I ran toward the forest. It didn't matter where I ran to, as long as I got away. Later, I would stop to figure out directions and where to go.

I was just two feet from the line of trees when a shock

hit me, freezing me. My muscles locked down and I let out a yelp as pain coursed through me, rendering me useless.

My vision darkened and my head swam in a black cloud of nothing.

I blinked, trying to make sense of what was going. What was I doing? Where I was?

Finally, the darkness covering my eyes retreated and I found myself looking up at a group of lesser demons, all of them snickering at me.

I pushed up to my paws, but my knees buckled and pain shot through me.

The demons hooked their arms around my limbs. I jerked against their hold, but I couldn't fight it. I didn't have any strength left.

The darkness took over me as they dragged me back inside the manor.

9

FARRAH

With a small lantern in my hand, I teleported to one of the bigger villages in the Wind Court. At this time of night, the market was closed, which was better for me. Careful not to be seen by the patrol guards, I sneaked into the marketplace and easily found wolfsbane and darkmallow.

But I couldn't find any faerend. I didn't think I would. Faerend was forbidden to be sold long ago, since it was highly toxic to our kind. As far as I knew, the plants from where this bud bloomed were all destroyed too.

Still, I had hoped some vendors would have a stash hidden to sell behind the authorities' backs. Or they hid it very well and I couldn't find it, or they really didn't have it.

Either way, I was out of luck.

Without any other ideas, I trudged into the forest to look for the plant. I had never seen it with my own eyes, but I knew it was a short bush with green, dried vines, and the small purple buds here and there.

The lamp I carried only illuminated so much, making my search harder and frustrating me more by the second. How would I find this damn plant if I could barely see anything?

Soon, the sun would rise and I had to be back to the Shade Fortress by then. If I wasn't, hell would break loose and I would be in big trouble.

My steps became faster as I combed the woods. I tripped on an overturned root and fallen branches every few seconds, but I didn't dare to slow down. I couldn't.

Suddenly, I heard shouts. I slowed down, thinking it was guards who were after me, but soon realized it wasn't. I stepped closer to the voices and light illuminated the night. I spied from under a tree and saw a deep valley in the middle of the forest, where a prison camp was hidden.

My heart squeezed as I watched the shadow fae guards yelling and whipping the fae prisoners.

I closed my eyes as a sudden rage washed through. No, I couldn't help these people, not now. If I did, chances were I would get caught, or I would help a few escape ... and then what? I would become a fugitive with them?

Though it hurt every muscle and instinct in my body, I turned away from the camp, promising myself I would help them later somehow.

Before, I was frustrated and in a hurry. Now I was also upset and shaken.

And to add to my dark emotions, the sun was beginning to rise.

I stopped and held the medallion in my hands, ready to go back to the Shade Fortress. Somehow, Jennie would have to steal it for me again and I would have to come back. Unless I found another way and—

"Hello there."

I quickly hid the medallion and called on my magic, ready to defend myself if necessary.

An older male fae stepped from between the trees, holding an orange cat. He had a small smile and curious eyes. He looked inoffensive, but I wouldn't take any chances.

I lifted my hand, ice enveloping it. "Stay back."

The fae stopped but didn't lose his smile. "No need to be alarmed. I'm Spencer and this is Rusty."

I took a step back, my arms still outstretched toward him. "What do you want?"

"Well, actually, I know you have been looking for something." He picked up a small cloth from inside his pocket, and while juggling the cat on his arms, he unfolded the cloth and showed me what was lying inside.

I gasped. "Faerend." I stared at him, shocked. "How did you know?"

He shrugged. "I'm just an old fae with a very good sixth sense."

I eyed the herb in his hands. "And you'll just give it to me."

He shook his head. "No, but I have a request."

I frowned. "What kind of request?"

"Though Rusty is a wildcat, he behaves like a house cat. He would be much more suited to live inside. Take him with you and care for him, and I'll give you the herb."

I stared at the old fae, baffled. Was this some kind of trick? "Take the cat … but that doesn't make sense."

"Sometimes things don't have to make sense." He extended his hand. "Do you want the herb or not?"

Shit, how could I pass this on? And all I had to do was take the cat with me. I would just drop him in my room and ask Jennie to feed him. It should be simple.

"Sure," I mumbled, still a little fazed about this turn of events. "I'll take the cat *and* the herb."

"Wonderful." As if we were old friends, Spencer dropped the cat in my arms. It was heavier and bigger than I anticipated, but the cat simply lay in my arms and rested his head on my chest, ready to take a cat. He also placed the herb in my hands. "Now you can go."

And just like that, the old fae turned around and walked away.

For a moment, all I could do was stare at the darkness between the trees where Spencer had disappeared through. What had just happened?

The first rays of sunlight streamed through the tall trees.

Shit, I had no time to wonder about that. With the cat in my arms and the herbs stashed in my pocket, I opened a portal back to my chambers in the Shade Fortress and stepped through.

10

I STIRRED ON THE COLD FLOOR, WAKING UP FROM ANOTHER nightmare. Gasping, I sat up and quickly looked around. I was still in the same fucking manor, in the same fucking room, with the same fucking chains around my wrists.

Well, not the same. Ever since I managed to escape almost two weeks ago, the demons didn't take any more chances. They enforced the chains and the only door in the room. They also fed me very little, just enough so I wouldn't starve, but certainly not enough for me to keep my strength. And every once in awhile, one of them came and tortured me. It mostly comprised of punches and shallow cuts, but in my already weakened state, it was enough to extract low howls of pain and sometimes to make me faint.

In these two weeks, Drollmor hadn't been back. I had asked what was going on, but the demons here didn't tell me anything. From the very little I overhead, Drollmor was still busy with the demon hunters. I really hoped it was Rey and Erin and that they were kicking Drollmor' ass so hard, the demon died by their hands.

One could only dream.

On the morning of the fifteenth day, a lesser demon brought me a slice of stale bread and half a cup of water.

"You should eat it all," he said, a sarcastic tone to his voice. "Drollmor is coming back tonight and when we tell him about your little escape, he'll torture you before taking your soul to the underworld."

I stilled, my stiffen limbs sore from barely moving for several days. Drollmor was coming back tonight? Fuck. My time was up. If I didn't escape now, then I would never escape again. No, by midnight, I would be dead and my soul would be forever lost to the depths of the underworld.

I jerked against my chains, in a vain attempt to break them. Laughing, the demon stepped out of my room and locked the door.

I ate the bread and drank the water, barely being able to hold on to things and take them to my mouth with the tight chains, but I needed all the strength I could get right now.

All day, I waited for the demons to come back and bring me more food. When they came, I would do something, anything. I would make one of them approach me and I would somehow wrap the chain around his neck. He would have the keys to my chains and I would escape.

But no one came.

Desperation was growing inside me when I heard

noises from outside. First, it seemed like someone ordering the demons around. After a few seconds, the noises grew closer and I heard better. It was the sound of shouts and a fight.

What the fuck was going on now?

Readying myself to shift and fight, I stood up on trembling legs.

The door burst open. Light and fire exploded from the hallway outside.

I gasped as the two of them stepped into the room.

"There you are," Ariella said with a small smile.

"You don't look too great," Kayden observed.

I collapsed to my knees. "I'm so fucking glad you're here."

"As you should be." Ariella rushed to me and started unlocking my chains with keys she probably got from the lesser demons. "Now let's go before the higher demon comes." She glanced at me. "Not that I don't want a turn with him, but in your state, we better go." She hooked her arm around mine and tugged me up. I swayed on my feet.

Kayden reached forward and caught my other arm, steadying me. "Hang in there."

I tried, but our escape from the manor was a blur in my mind. I saw as Ariella used her powers to kill a couple of demons as we left the manor, I saw as Kayden used her powers to set fire to the manor, and I saw as the both of them pushed me on the backseat of a car.

And then I didn't remember anything else.

WHEN I WOKE UP, I WAS IN A SOFT BED IN A SIMPLE ROOM. Sunlight streamed from the closed drapes, and the smell of coffee reached my nose.

I sat up, groaning at my sore muscles and dizzy head. My stomach contracted with hunger. I glanced down at myself. Though my face was clean, my hair was plastered to my head, and I still wore the last clothes the demons had given me after I ripped the previous outfit when I shifted.

I was in desperate need of a bath, but I was even more so for food.

Following the scent of coffee, I exited the room, walked through a small hallway, and found a family room with an open kitchen. Ariella and Kayden had mugs in their hands and ate something with cinnamon. The sweet scent was killing me!

"Sleeping beauty is up," Kayden said. She gestured to the coffeemaker across the kitchen, then to the plate with cinnamon scones on top of the range. "Help yourself."

With slow steps, I made my way to the kitchen, grabbed some coffee and a lot of scones, and sat down on one of the stools around the kitchen's tall stools, right beside Ariella.

"Where are we?" I asked, confused.

"A house on the east coast, near the Shade Fortress," Ariella said. "The couple living here went to Europe for vacation."

I frowned and glanced out the window, but didn't see much. "What about the neighbors. Won't they see the house occupied?"

She shook her head. "The next house is down the road, and many trees surround all lots." She narrowed her eyes at me. "How are you feeling?"

"I'm not dead," I joked, though it hurt to smile, much less to laugh. I let out a long sigh, but even that was painful. "I've been better."

"I can see that."

"How did you find me?" I asked, my mouth full of scone. I was inhaling them, though I was sure I would get sick later since my stomach wasn't used to eating this much, this fast anymore.

"It was hard," Kayden said. "We had no clue, no idea what had happened."

"Kayden is a great tracker," Ariella said, sounding proud for some reason. "After many days following endless trails, she found you in that manor." Ariella narrowed her blue eyes at me. "What happened? What did those demons want with you?"

I swallowed the last bite of my scone. "Remember I told you I've got mixed up with a demon? Yeah, he found me. His name is Drollmor."

"What did you do to them to have them come after you in a camp full of fae?" Ariella asked.

I let out a long breath. I could lie to her, but was that worth it? I didn't see why. I was so fucking tired of lies. "Drollmor promised me I would find Farrah again and would be with her if I sold my soul to him."

Ariella looked at me as if I had told her I had kissed the devil. "No ..." she mumbled, shaking her head. "You didn't. You're not that stupid."

"I was lost, I was scared, I didn't have a life, in fact, I thought about dying all the fucking time," I explained. Though now that I said those things out loud, they didn't sound like a good reason. "I don't know. He found me when I was at my lowest and he made me a deal that seemed like it could change my luck, despite the outcome."

"I can't believe you're that stupid," Ariella said, her eyes shining with disgust. She hated demons with a vengeance, and now that she found out I had sold my soul to one, she probably hated me just as much.

"It's done," I snapped, though I regretted it. I could have found Farrah by myself if I had only stopped mopping and done something about it. "All I can do now is run from him and hope he never catches up."

Ariella stood from the table and took several steps back. "I'm not sure I can help you anymore."

What? "You have to!" I rose from my seat but didn't approach her. "If you don't help me, help us, we can't take the shadow prince down. We need to rescue Farrah. Please."

She glanced at me as if I was a bug that didn't deserve living. I understood how bad all of this sounded to her, but fuck it, she had to understand. At the time, I had no other choice. It was that, or simply die at the streets, killed by demons in a senseless death.

"I'll help you, but for Farrah, not for you," she said, her tone hard. "But you have to promise me one thing, though. When we rescue Farrah and we're all safe, you're going to tell her about it."

Fuck. Did I have to? Right now, I would promise

anything. I might even sell my soul again if that meant getting Farrah back.

"I promise."

11

FARRAH

FOR THE PAST TWO WEEKS, I BREWED THE POTION IN MY closet. Jennie helped me with it since the faerend in the potion dulled my powers and made me weak. She didn't mind when it affected her.

Thankfully, the few times Lark came into my chambers, he never wandered far, much less into my closet. Even so, I was always nervous that for some reason, he would start looking around too much and find the potion.

Once he asked about the bitter scent in my room. I lied to him it was the new tea Jennie had been bringing to me. He didn't ask about it anymore.

But he did ask about the cat.

"I don't know where it came from," I told him one night, trying to sound innocent. "I came back from the library one day and it was just here." I ran my hand over the cat's fluffy fur and the cat stretched under my touch. "I didn't send him away because I enjoy the company."

Though he frowned looking at the cat, Lark let that subject go.

Unlike when fae from other courts came into the fortress for a diplomatic dinner, and Lark wanted me to join him. I begged him not to go, telling him I wasn't feeling well, but he wouldn't have it.

"You're my wife, and you'll be my mate. You have to be there. It's non-negotiable," he insisted, his tone not leaving room for arguments.

And that was how I ended up in a black gown with a tight corset and flowy skirt, and a long slit along my right leg. My long white-blonde hair was pinned behind my head, so the gown's deep V showed off my bare back. The gown was beautiful, but I felt naked, exposed, paraded like a pretty piece of jewelry.

Lark waited for me behind the closed doors to the main hall. The diplomats were all inside and he wanted to make a grand entrance. He held my hand in his and when the doors opened and we stepped inside, I felt like this was our second wedding.

Though this time I was wearing black. Could it be my funeral?

As I expected, Lark walked slowly, turning me this way and that way, showing off his trophy wife. I plastered a weak smile on my lips and just went with it.

Soon, this would all be over. Soon, I would kill him and that would be the end of this farce.

After greetings, where I met several fae from all the courts in the fae realm—except for frost fae—Lark directed us all to the dining room, where a feast had been prepared.

I sat beside Lark at the head of the table, while the others took the many chairs along the table. No one sat on the other end of the table.

Dinner progressed as expected: boring as the fae talk about politics and lowly humans, and other races. Some were appalled that they had to come to the human world to meet with Lark, others were stunned the prince was still living here.

To be honest, I was too.

As a show to his guests, Lark reached to me and put his hand over my leg, slipping his hand around my thigh, dangerously close to my groin.

I squirmed as far as I could in my chair, but he closed his hand around my thigh, digging his fingers into my skin. I swallowed the yelp that threatened to escape.

All around us, the fae continued with their conversation, though their eyes shifted from our faces to Lark's touch.

His hand hiked up, and just before it went too far, I crossed my legs and turned my body to the side, reaching for my wine goblet with too much fanfare. Lark had to drop his hand.

The guests noticed my move but didn't say anything.

To his credit, Lark tried to keep going as normal, but his pride was hurt.

A minute later, he shot up. "Excuse us," he said through gritted teeth. He pulled me behind him across the dining room and into the hallway. He let go of my hand

and turned his furious eyes to me. "What the hell do you think you're doing?"

I lifted my chin. "We may be married, but I'm not yours."

"You are mine," he hissed. "You will be mine. You better start realizing and soon, because when the Moon Period is over in another week, you *will* be mine."

A chill ran down my spine.

Not if I killed you first, you scumbag.

I didn't say anything, because if I opened my mouth, I would say things that would only put me in more trouble.

Lark glared at me. "You're dismissed. Go back to your chambers."

This time, I was glad to obey him. I simply turned around and marched along the hallway, going back to my bedroom.

Soon, I would be free from this place. Free from him.

12

WYATT

FROM A DISTANCE, WE WATCHED THE SHADE FORTRESS rising up to the sky along the side of the mountain. If we got closer, we would run into patrols and right now we couldn't afford to do that.

"To get to the prince and rescue Farrah, we need to get inside," I said. "But the place is too well guarded."

"I can glamour us as servants so we can sneak in," Kayden said, her eyes on the fortress. "It won't last long, but it should be enough to get us inside."

I nodded. "Then, once inside we should split up. I'll go find Farrah, while you two find the prince." I glanced at Ariella. She was still ignoring me.

"Sounds like a plan," Kayden said. "We should sneak in early tomorrow morning, during the guard change." I had been out for a couple of days, and during that time, Kayden studied the movements outside the fortress. "What do you think?"

I nodded again, sure I needed another good night sleep

before sneaking inside a fortress and probably having to fight for my life, and for Farrah's life. Actually, I doubted I would be able to sleep, but at least I could stay in bed and let my body rest.

That night, we went back to our borrowed house near the fortress. After a quiet dinner, Ariella made tea and retreated to her bedroom.

Kayden poured some tea in two mugs and brought it to the living room, where I was seated on the couch, too worked up to relax and try to rest.

"Here," she said, offering one of the mugs to me. "It should help you relax."

I took the steaming mug from her. "Thank you."

Kayden sat down on an armchair across from me. After a moment of silence, she asked, "So, tell me, why is this frost fae so important to you?"

I stared into my mug, wondering what I should tell her. But why lie to her? She was here, after all, and willing to help us, help me. "I've known Farrah for three years now. I've always loved her, since the first moment I saw her, left beaten up by witches in a forest." I drank a sip of my tea. "And recently I found out she's my mate. Though, I know about the curse the fae king put on the fae. She can never love me otherwise she will lose her immortality."

Kayden scoffed. "Immortality is overrated. If she is your mate, if she really loves you, she should choose to have a life with you, to grow old and die with you."

For some reason, I didn't tell her that I wasn't sure if Farrah knew she was my mate. We hadn't talked about that before she left me and married the evil fae prince.

"I'm not going to force her to choose between me and her immortality."

Kayden dropped her mug in the low coffee table in between us. "I understand. Perhaps I just talk about immortality as if it wasn't a big deal, because my people and I have been living in the human realm for a long time. Soon, we'll lose our powers, and our immortality too. I've already come to terms with it."

That picked my interest. Besides, it was an interesting subject to take my mind off Farrah for a few minutes. "How did the blaze fae end up here?"

"Alos, my father, used to be king of the fae," she said, her tone bitter. "He was a good king, but he trusted easily. One of his advisors set him up, a web so intricate, no one saw it until it was too late. He almost killed my father, but I was able to steal him away from the castle before that happened. The shadow king killed most blaze fae, so we ended up fleeing the fae realm all together." She paused. "I felt like a coward running like that, but I couldn't just stand there and watch my people get killed."

"You planned on attacking back."

I wasn't asking, but she nodded all the same. "At first, I thought we would regroup, get stronger, and fight back. But our numbers were small, and our fae became afraid of the power of the shadow king. So we ended up just settling here, hidden in that canyon." She lifted her amber eyes to me. "Until you came to ask for help."

I nodded. "Still, it's just that three of us against a fortress full of shadow fae."

"If we plan it right, we can do it." The conviction in her

gaze, in her voice, stirred something in me. I wanted to believe in her more than I believed in my own wishes.

"After Alos, you would be the fae queen." Again, I didn't ask, but Kayden confirmed with a bob of her chin. "I'll do everything I can to help you restore your throne."

It was a promise and I hoped to keep this one.

13

Not long after that failed dinner party Lark threw to his diplomats, the poison was ready. In the middle of the night, I carefully poured some of the poison into a glass vial and put it inside my pocket.

It was late, but I knew that tonight, Lark was busy with a new diplomat who had come to speak with him from the fae realm. He would be late to his chambers. I could easily lie I wanted to see her, to wait for him at his chambers, and slip the poison into his wine, the one he drank day and night, proclaiming it was energizing.

In the morning, he would wake up, drink a sip, and fall dead.

I snuck out of my chambers, relieved Lark thought the fortress was already well guarded and hadn't ordered guards to stay outside my doors. I walked down the hallways, avoiding the patrols and areas where I knew guards were positioned.

Though, as I rounded a corner just before the stairs that led to the fortress's highest floor, where Lark's chambers, were located, voices reached my ears.

I stilled, afraid of being discovered.

"... soldier came back a few hours ago," a voice said. I recognized it. It was General Auron. "The camp is secure, and the frost fae are all submissive as planned."

My stomach dropped. *What?*

"Good," someone else said. It was one of Lark's advisors. "I knew they wouldn't rebel for long. They can't. They have nowhere to go. How about Daleigh?"

"He was beaten up into submission. I don't think he'll be a problem, at least for a while."

I pressed a hand over my mouth as shock and rage mixed within me.

"With him down, the other frost fae won't do anything," the advisor continued. "They will be quiet, little prisoners, as they should be."

My hands curled into fists. I wanted to storm out of my hiding place, lunge on these two fae, and kill them on the spot.

So Lark had lied to me. He had said Daleigh and the other frost fae had returned home and were free. Well, they had returned home, but now they were all imprisoned in a prison camp.

My rage took the best of me and I advanced, intent on torturing them both, and ripping every one of their muscles while they screamed and begged me to stop, and—

Footsteps sounded from behind me. I quickly ducked

under an archway and quietly opened a door, which I knew led to an empty guest bedroom. I closed the door and waited, listening for the steps and the voices to fade away.

My heart racing, my vision swimming in red fury, I leaned my back against the wall beside the door and tried to calm down.

But I couldn't. I wouldn't calm down, not entirely. I clutched the vial with poison inside my pocket. Now more than ever, I wanted to kill the damn fae prince. It wasn't just because I couldn't stand staying by his side for eternity anymore. It was for his lies, for my people, for everything!

He was just as evil as his father.

And he would die tonight.

I waited a while longer inside the bedroom, until I was sure the guards and the others had moved on. Then I continued my trek to Lark's chambers. Thankfully, when I arrived there, no one was standing outside his door, which meant he was still somewhere else in the fortress.

I reached for the knob and twisted it. I gasped in surprise when the door opened. I was actually expecting it would be locked and I would have to use my powers to unlock it.

Counting my blessings, I tiptoed in his bedroom and found the bottle of wine waiting for him on the side table of a large, leather armchair on a corner of the room. Holding my breath, I opened the vial and poured the poison in the wine. I sniffed it, making sure the scent wasn't detectable. It wasn't.

With a small smile, I left his chambers and sneaked back into my own.

Now all I had to do was wait.

By tomorrow morning, the fae prince would be dead.

14

THE SUN WAS RISING WHEN ARIELLA, KAYDEN, AND I donned glamour of servants, waited for the change of guards, and sneaked into the fortress.

That had been easier than I thought it would be, but it hadn't been the first time we had done something similar. When Farrah, Luana, and I had come to find the Dagger of All Hunting three years ago, we had entered the fortress much in the same way.

The problem wasn't really getting in the fortress. The problem was getting the fuck out.

But I wouldn't worry about that now. Now, all I cared about was finding Farrah.

As soon as we arrived in the servants' wing inside the fortress, Ariella and Kayden went to one side, and I went to another.

"Good luck," I whispered to them, before parting ways.

Ariella didn't even glance my way. I couldn't blame her. I wasn't mad that she was mad at me. I was just upset. In the time we had spent together, I had come to consider her a friend. And now I had lost her.

Hopefully, she would come around once all of this fucking mess was done.

I shook my head, clearing my thoughts, and focused on the problem at hand. As a servant, I made my way up the stairs, into the main level of the fortress. I tensed as I walked by a set of patrols, but no one stopped me.

I let out a long breath of relief.

Until another male fae stepped into my way. "What are you doing here?" He wore a uniform like a servant's one, but his was more elaborate. His ranking among the servants was higher. "All servants are to report to the court-yard immediately." He grabbed my arm and pulled me along with him.

I started protesting but decided against it. If I fought this fae now, it would only make everything worse. I went along with him, at least until I figured out what was happening. He brought me back downstairs into the servants' wing and shoved me into a large courtyard where many other servants stood, all looking confused. Guards flanked the walls, all looking ready to attack if necessary.

What the fuck was happening here?

The male fae turned his attention to the servants. "Someone tried to poison the prince last night," he said, his voice loud enough to carry through the courtyard. Gasps of surprise filled the air. I frowned. "No one leaves this courtyard until everyone is fully investigated." He gestured to a young female fae just a few steps from him. "You're going first."

With her head low, the female fae approached the male. He pulled her to the back of the courtyard. Just then General Auron stepped into the courtyard. My insides chilled. Even though I was glamoured, I glanced down, afraid he would recognize me.

From under my lashes, I watched for a few moments, while General Auron interrogated the young female fae, then dismissed her and called another servant.

Fuck. I couldn't be investigated. It would either break my glamour, or they would realize they had never seen a servant who looked like me before.

I had to get the fuck out of here right now, but guards were stationed along the walls, every ten feet or so.

With my werewolf agility, I reached into the pocket of one fae and snatched the first thing I grabbed—a thick, golden coin. I stopped for a second, wondering who the fuck had a gold coin, and why, but I honestly didn't care. Instead, I acted on the rest of my plan. I dropped the coin among the feet of a male fae with a wild demeanor.

It took less time than I thought it would. The first fae realized her coin was gone and started shouting she had been robbed. She saw the coin at the other fae's feet and accused him of stealing her.

Chaos ensued and several guards from along the walls stepped forward to check what was happening.

And I slipped from one of the courtyard's archways and disappeared inside the fortress.

15

I JOLTED OUT OF BED AS THE DOORS TO MY CHAMBERS BURST open.

"What is going on?" I asked, sitting up. I was glad I had chosen a moderate nightgown for tonight, knowing I would be awoken once they found Lark's body.

The cat let out a shriek and jumped off my bed, where it had been sleeping at my feet, and disappeared from sight just as four soldiers walked in my room, then parted ways, standing guard on the side. A moment later, Prince Lark strode in my chambers. What ... I schooled my expression to remain cool, lest he saw the shock now coursing through me.

"My dear Farrah," he said as he halted just a couple of feet from me. "Someone tried to poison me a couple of hours ago."

"W-what?" I willed my voice to be surprised by such revelation. "What happened?"

"I had company," the prince explained, his tone

amused. He thought I didn't know he still took innocent female fae to his bedroom almost every night? "She drank from my wine before me, and within seconds, she was dead at my feet."

I put a hand over my mouth. "That's horrible."

"I agree." The prince nodded. "The fact is someone inside this castle tried to poison me and we're intent on investigating everyone until we find the culprit." His dark eyes held on mine. "You wouldn't mind if my guards searched your bedroom, would you?"

"Of course not." I gestured wide. "Go ahead." I mentally gave myself a pat on the back for having gotten rid of everything before I went to bed last night.

The four soldiers rummaged around my chambers, looking under and behind every piece of furniture and painting and other decorations. They searched my bathroom and my closet.

And found nothing.

Prince Lark tsked. "I'm so sorry I doubted of you," he said, his voice almost earnest. He snapped his fingers and a male fae was brought into my room, being held by the arms by another two soldiers.

I stood up as the fae's desperate eyes met mine. "Who is this?"

"My winemaker," Lark explained. "I've been searching for a while now, and I can't find anyone who would want to poison me. Thus, the winemaker must have put the poison in my wine himself."

"My prince, it wasn't me!" the fae shouted. "I wouldn't have! I—"

I gasped in horror as Lark moved his arm as fast as lightning and slashed the winemaker's throat with a dagger I didn't even see he was holding. A gurgled sound came from the fae's mouth and blood seeped from his throat.

First the poor female fae who drank the wine, now the winemaker. Two fae had died because of my plan. Because of me.

Prince Lark turned to me, his face serene, as if he hadn't just killed a fae in cold blood. He took another step closer to me and I did my best to hold my ground. I couldn't show him how much I was disgusted with him, how much I feared him.

He reached for my hand and held my arm. He clasped a black stone bracelet around my wrist. "A gift for my wife," he said in a honeyed tone.

I glanced down at the bracelet, stunned. What the hell was he doing? "Thank you," I whispered, still in shock.

Lark placed a kiss on my cheek. "Sorry to have bothered you. I'll let you go back to bed while my soldiers and I resume our investigation."

With that, the soldiers dragged the winemaker's body from the room, leaving a trail of blood on the floor. Everyone walked out and the doors closed with a finite click behind them.

I stood there in absolute horror for a few moments, trying to gather my wits.

I knew Prince Lark was evil, but I hadn't realized he was more than that. He was insane and evil, and he liked it. My skin crawled with revulsion and fright.

I had to get out of here. I couldn't stay here as a victim, especially now that I knew Lark had lied to me and imprisoned my brother and my people, instead of letting them go as he had promised me. I had to get out of here and find a way to go back to the fae realm to save my people.

After waiting a few minutes, I changed my nightgown for sensible clothes—black leather pants, a thin sweater, and boots.

As I left my bedroom, careful not to step in the blood smearing the stone floors, the sun was going up outside the window. Hopefully, the hallways would be still dark and since the soldiers were all following Lark wherever he was going, I would be able to slip through the fortress unnoticed.

To my relief, I made it to the outer wall of the fortress just fine. But there were two guards standing in front of the gates leading outside. I quickly put a glamour over me, disguising as another fae guard. I didn't have to interact with them. All I had to was cross the gates.

Then I would run like a mad woman until I was far away from here.

My plan worked well, until the moment I took one step past the gates.

Pain shot straight from my core, making me double over and my vision too blurry. I was about to fall on my knees when one of the guards snatched my arms.

"Are you okay?" he asked, his tone not that caring. He pulled me back a little, and the pain was gone.

What the ...

I disentangled myself from him and stepped forward again.

The pain came back, hitting me harder this time. I not only doubled over, but I fell on my knees and threw up.

"What is going on with you?" the other guard asked me, eyeing me with repulsion.

Groaning, I scooted back inside the fortress.

The pain was gone and I inhaled deeply, savoring the reprieve.

Baffled, I looked down at the bracelet on my wrist and I suddenly realized what was going on. The bracelet wasn't a gift from Lark, it was a curse. If I tried to leave, the magic in the bracelet was activated. If I really left, it would kill me.

I was stuck here forever.

16

EXITING THE COURTYARD WAS EASY. THE PROBLEM NOW WAS to navigate the fortress without being caught, since all the servants were supposed to be at the courtyard, being interrogated for what happened to prince Lark.

Someone tried poisoning the prince. That sent the wheels of my mind turning, but I really didn't have fucking time to think about him and what that could mean. I had to find Farrah as soon as possible.

Luck struck on my side when a young female fae crossed my path. She was dressed in the servant's uniform and she wasn't locked in the courtyard with the others.

"Excuse me," I said, wondering how would a fae servant talk to another. It didn't matter now. "Hm, I'm new here and I was sent to check on the princess, though I've been getting easily lost around the fortress. Could you please tell me the way to her chambers?"

She eyed me with wariness, but after a short hesitation, she pointed down the hallway and gave me directions to the third floor. I thanked her and rushed through the hallways, following her directions.

At the landing of the third floor, I bumped into two fae guards.

Momentarily caught off guard, their reaction time was slow. So I acted faster.

I pounced on one of the guards, swiped his spear from him, and pushed it into his chest, across his heart. The second guard was already on me, his spear coming for my back. Wishing I had time to shift into my wolf, I spun to the side, missing the spear's blade by one inch. But I didn't stop. I moved my arm up, punching the spear, making the fae loose his grip on it. I grabbed it hard and landed a nice elbow strike on the fae's nose. He dropped his hands to touch his nose, and I turned the spear around, the blade pointed at him. Before he could react, I drove the spear through his neck.

A gurgling noise came from his throat right before his body thudded on the floor.

I dragged the bodies into the nearest room. I cleaned my hands on the tunic of one of the guards, then stole the pants and shirt of the other one. I didn't forget about the stone I was carrying and tucked it safely away in my pocket. Hoping my glamour was still in place after this fight, I slipped from the room and continued on my path.

It didn't take long for me to find the double doors at the end of the hallway—Farrah's bedroom.

My heart started beating faster as I turned the knob and pushed the door open. My breath caught as my eyes found her.

Heartbreakingly beautiful as always, Farrah stood before the large window on the other side of the room, the warm light from the sunrise kissing her porcelain skin and silver hair.

She turned wary eyes at me. "Who are you?"

I closed and locked the door. "Lift my glamour," I told her.

Frowning, she waved her hands, using her magic to turn off my glamour. I felt the moment the magic slipped away from me.

Farrah's bright blue eyes went wide. "Wyatt," she whispered in disbelief.

I stood there, watching her, afraid of moving. But she moved first. She launched herself in my arms. With a deep inhale, I held her tight against me, relishing in the feeling of her with me, in her scent filling my nostrils.

Then she stiffened and pulled back to look at me. "What are you doing here?"

I held on to her arms, refusing to let her put distance between us. "I came for you, to rescue from this place."

The defeated shine in her eyes squeezed at my heart. "I can't." She lifted her arm and showed me the black bracelet in her wrist. "Lark put this on me earlier today. I tried escaping after. This bracelet will kill me if I leave the fortress." I grabbed her arm and tried pulling the bracelet off. She shook her head. "I've already tried that and more. The bracelet is enchanted. It won't come off."

"There must be a way," I whispered. "I can't leave my mate trapped here."

Her eyes rounded for a moment, then a small smile appeared over her lips. "You felt it too?"

I nodded. "I wasn't sure if you had." I pulled her back to me. "Farrah, I love you. I have always loved you. I can't let you stay here."

Gently, Farrah cupped my face, and standing on tiptoes, she pressed her lips to mine. I groaned, not content with just a peck. I closed my mouth over hers and kissed her, showing her just how much I wanted her, I needed her, I loved her.

Farrah kissed me back, moving her lips in rhythm with mine, her tongue entwining with mine. I wrapped my arms around her, like a lock that wouldn't break, no matter what.

But then Farrah stepped back, breaking our kiss before I could take it further. "Wyatt, you need to go. It's not safe here. You'll be found out and killed."

I held to her hand. "I won't leave you."

She pressed a hand to my chest. "You need to. Listen to me. Lark lied. He didn't let Daleigh and my people go. They are imprisoned somewhere in the fae realm. Go there. Find them, free them. Rescue Daleigh. I know he'll be mad now and will want vengeance. He'll know what to do."

A wave of rage coursed for me. That fucking fae prince ... I sucked in a deep breath, trying to stay calm. I would lose my temper, but not now. Later, when I faced off the prince. I would put an end to him. But right now, I had to stay levelheaded. Even though I didn't like it, Farrah seemed to know what she was saying. If she trusted Daleigh for this, I would too.

I nodded. "I hate leaving you, but I'll go after Daleigh. Then we'll come back for you." I leaned into her and kissed her deep and hard one more time. "I promise it," I whispered against her lips.

"Now go," she said, pushing me toward the door.

Reluctantly, I let go of her. But as I was turning from her, I remembered something. "Oh, I have something for you." I pulled the blue pendant Spencer had given me from my pocket and handed it to her.

She took the blue stone "What is this?"

I shrugged. "I don't know. I just promised I would give it to you."

17

FARRAH

ONE HOUR AFTER WYATT LEFT, I FINALLY STOPPED CRYING. Seeing my mate, touching him, and not being able to leave with him was not only heartbreaking, but it was also slowly killing me.

Staying here would kill me.

But if I tried to leave, I would be dead too.

I waited another hour to compose myself before I tried leaving my room. I couldn't escape this fortress, but nothing could stop me from going to the library and research about this damn bracelet. If there had been books about poison, I was sure there would be books about magical objects. Hopefully, there would be one about this specific one and I would be able to take it off.

But a surprise waited for me when I opened the doors of my chambers. Four guards stood there, blocking my way.

"What is going on?" I asked, alarmed. "When did you get here?" Had they seen Wyatt leaving?

One of the soldiers turned to me and gave me a slight bow of his head. "Just a few minutes ago, your highness. Prince Lark asked us to keep you safe in your chambers while the investigation goes on."

I frowned. "So I can't leave my room?"

"For your own safety, no."

I scoffed. For my own safety—what a freaking lie. Lark was keeping me prisoner in here, probably another punishment since he knew I had been the one to slip poison into his wine. He might not have proof, but he knew.

Seething, I retreated into my chambers and closed the doors again. Damn it. I couldn't even wander inside the fortress. What the hell would I do now?

I didn't have to wait for long. A few minutes later, Jennie entered the room. "You're having lunch with the prince," she said, her tone quieter than usual.

"Are you okay?" I asked, worried about her. Had the prince beaten her up again?

Jennie lifted her sad eyes to me. "It's just ... General Auron and the soldiers are conducting an investigation to find out who tried to poison the prince."

I watched her for any indication that she had connected the dots. That she had realized the potion she helped me brew in my closet wasn't a fertility potion, but rather the poison used to try to kill the prince. But there was nothing in her gaze, no emotion. She was either even more naive than I thought, or she was a very good actress.

"And?" I asked, afraid of her next words."

"They are being rougher and crueler than usual," she said with a long sigh.

My stomach tightened. She and the other servants were suffering in the hands of Lark and his evil fae because of me. What other bad consequences my plan would have?

I followed Jennie into my closet and let her dress me in a beautiful black gown with a deep cleavage despite being just the middle of the day. In silence, she applied a little makeup to my face, and pulled my silver hair into an intricate braid behind my head.

If I didn't know better, I would think I was going to a ball in the middle of the day.

The guards escorted me to the dining room, where Lark waited for me, standing beside the long table, wearing a fancy suit and a thick cloak over his shoulder.

He smiled when he saw me. "You look beautiful."

I gave him a curtsy. "Thank you."

The guards stepped out of the room, giving us a little privacy. Lark gestured for me to approach him. He pulled up a chair at the end of the table and helped me sit down. Then he walked the length of the table and took the chair at the other end.

Servants came in with our lunch and drinks. Meanwhile, Lark talked to me about random things—the weather, a big battle against demon hunters and demons in the middle of the country, some unquiet witches who seemed to be stirring up trouble not far from here, and finally, his investigation.

By then, the servants had already brought dessert.

With the spoon in my hand, I picked on the fragrant chocolate cake, but I didn't feel like eating when Lark's dark eyes gained a somber glint.

He pushed up from his chair and stalked toward me. He grabbed the chair to my right and turned it toward me. He sat on it and leaned closer to me. "Let's stop playing games," he said, his tone cold. "I know it was you who put the poison in the wine."

My breath caught. I knew he knew, but I didn't think he would actually say it to my face. I preserved my honor and didn't deny it. Instead, I lifted my chin. "And?"

"The servant and the winemaker were warnings," he continued. "If you continue in this fool's quest of killing me or leaving this place, more fae will die. You'll just be leaving a string of bodies behind you." He reached over and ran his fingertips along my arms. What was supposed to be seductive, felt disgusting, and brought fear to my core. "You belong to me, Farrah, and you'll never be able to escape. You should have understood that by now." He leaned even closer, his breath washing against my shoulder. I suppressed a shudder. "In a couple of days, the moon period will be over, and after you're pregnant, I know you won't be going anywhere." He placed a hand over my belly. I tensed. "Not when I can use our child as leverage."

I snapped my face to him. He would use a child to blackmail me in behaving? More than ever, I was glad I couldn't have Lark's children.

Finally, he pulled back, a wicked half grin in his lips. "You're excused to go." He gestured to the doors. "Just know that you aren't allowed to go anywhere in the fortress without guard supervision. And you'll be kept locked in your chambers at all times, except for when I call on you." He waved his hand dismissing me. "Now go."

For a moment, I couldn't move. All I could do was stare at him, at his wickedness, at his pleasure in being so evil. Then I forced myself to move. I would rather stay locked in my room than anywhere near this vicious prince.

I stood and walked to the door without sparing him a word or a glance. The moment I stepped out of the dining room, four guards flanked me. I didn't pause, I didn't acknowledge them. I just kept moving, trying not to break down as hopelessness filled my heart.

With a heavy sigh, I entered my room and stood just behind the door, listening as it was closed and locked, the clicking sound echoing in my ears.

Now all I could do was wait and pray that Wyatt found Daleigh and they came up with a magnificent plan to rescue me.

18

AFTER LEAVING FARRAH'S CHAMBERS, I FOUND ARIELLA AND Kayden rushing through the corridors.

"What happened?" I asked, confused with their worried eyes.

"We failed," Kayden said, her tone flat. "We couldn't even get close to the prince with this poisoning attempt."

Ariella glanced behind me. "Where's Farrah?"

My shoulders sagged and I shook my head. "She can't come."

"What?" she almost shrieked.

"I'll explain when we're out of here," I pressed. I looked around. "How we're going to leave this place?"

Kayden waved her hands and I felt the jolt of magic coursing over my skin. "We're all guards now. Better make our way to the nearest gate and run."

We did exactly that, and with all of the soldiers' attention on the poisoning investigation, it was easy enough to fool them and exit the fortress.

Once we were far enough, Kayden withdrew our glamour. And when we stepped inside the house we were borrowing, Ariella turned to me.

"Now explain," she said, her tone as cold as her silver eyes.

I let out a long sigh and explained about the bracelet the prince had clasped around Farrah's wrist and what happened when she tried leaving. Then I told them about the Daleigh and the other frost fae.

"Prince Lark went back on his word," I continued. "He imprisoned Daleigh and the others in the fae realm. They are back in the fae realm, but they aren't free."

Ariella cursed under her breath. "So, what? We're going to rescue them?"

"That's what Farrah asked," I said. "She thinks Daleigh and the frost fae can help us. With their numbers, we can invade the fortress and defeat the shadow prince and his soldiers."

Kayden started pacing in the middle of the living room. "That wasn't what I signed up for. The agreement was to come here and deal with the shadow prince right away."

"I know, but unfortunately, things changed." I looked at her, hoping she saw how fucking desperate I was. "Please, take us to the fae realm and help us free the frost fae."

Kayden stopped facing and closed her eyes tight. She groaned, then returned her eyes to me. "All right."

It wasn't hard to find the frost fae and their prison camp. By now, the entire fae realm had heard about the camp, since it was used as an example, showing all fae what would happen to them if they didn't behave as they were expected to.

We hid behind the top of a hill and spied out the clearing ahead, where a large prison held out the frost fae. The cages were probably eight to nine feet high, and hundreds of feet wide, divided into sections I couldn't make out yet. From here, all I could see was that the frost fae was separated into three groups, all in the west corner of the cages, while shadow fae patrolled the inside and the outside of the prison.

"How many shadow fae?" Ariella asked.

"Too many," Kayden said.

"Anyone have a good plan?" I asked.

"There won't be a good plan, but I have a half-assed one," Kayden said. "Ariella and I will go to the west side of the prison and create a distraction. Most of the guards should go our way. Then you sneak into the prison and free the frost fae."

I frowned. "How will I sneak into the prison?"

She grabbed a small rock from the ground and wrapped her hand around it. An orange shine peeked from in between her fingers. After, she ripped a corner of her tunic, wrapped the stone in it, and offered it to me. "Press it against a lock, or even a metal bar. It'll melt and you'll be able to get in."

I got the stone from her.

After a quick nod of agreement, Kayden and Ariella

ran out, rounding the hill and going to the other side of the camp.

Keeping myself hidden behind tall blades of grass and bushes, I approached the prison as much as could and waited.

I was starting to think both women had been caught when I finally heard it.

An explosion coming from the other side of the prison.

19

ALL I COULD DO WAS PACE AROUND MY BEDROOM AND HOPE for a miracle. Despite knowing better, I stopped every few minutes and tried pulling the damn bracelet off my wrist. And each time, it remained intact.

I scoffed. Why did I even bother trying? I knew it wouldn't come off so easily. If only I could go to the library and research some books.

The cat meowed, giving me a fright. Sometimes, I forgot he was even here, the damn animal. All he did was slumber on the armchair in the corner of the bedroom, or over my own pillow. At least, he was easy to care for.

Suddenly, the doors opened and Jennie entered my chambers, her head low. "Good afternoon, your highness," she said in a meek voice, her eyes to the floor.

I frowned. "Jennie, look at me." She flinched but lifted her head. I gasped at the new purple bruise on her temple and neck. I clenched my fists. "Did Prince Lark do this to you?" Jennie remained quiet. "You don't need to defend him, you know. If he hurt you, tell me."

She blinked, tears appearing at the corner of her eyes. "I shouldn't talk like that about him, your highness. It's wrong."

Why the hell was she still afraid of talking shit about him? He beat her up. She had to hate him. How could I make her see just how wrong he was and get her to help me without actually telling her the truth?

There was a way she could help me.

"Jennie, I would like to go to the library," I said, my voice firm.

"But the prince said—"

"I know the prince ordered me to stay in my room, but I would like you to go to him and tell him I'm bored out of my mind. I want new reading material and I would like a couple of hours at the library to choose a few books for myself." I gestured to the closed doors. "What's the worst that could happen if the guards will follow me there?"

Jennie hesitated, but she lowered her head. "Yes, my princess."

She left the room, and I started pacing again.

EITHER THE PRINCE WAS MORE GULLIBLE THAN HE SEEMED, or Jennie had been very convincing when telling him about my boredom. I didn't really care about how she persuaded him to let me come to the library, all that mattered was that I was here now, surrounded by the tall shelves and thousands of books.

The four guards had entered the library with me, but they stayed by the entranced, their eyes following every one of my movements.

I started browsing the fiction section, trying to throw my guards off. I picked two books from there, as decoy. Slowly, I made my way deeper into the library, to the back shelves where the books in magical objects were.

My heartbeat sped up as I searched through the books as fast as I could, always maintaining the fiction books on top, so if I was caught, I could hide the others. I skimmed through the books, searching for anything in this damn bracelet. I needed to find a way to get this shit off my wrist.

One hour passed and dozens of books had been searched, and I hadn't found anything about the bracelet. My nerves started to flare up in the second hour of my search. What if I didn't find anything? What if I could never take this bracelet off? Even if Wyatt came back with Daleigh, they wouldn't be able to rescue me.

My despair only grew with every minute.

Until I found something I didn't expect to.

As I was skimming a thick book about magical jewels, I stumbled on a smooth blue stone pendant. Frowning, I fished the blue stone Wyatt had given me from my pocket. I had asked him why he was giving me that, and he said he didn't know. I was given no other explanation before his time was tight and he had to sneak out of the fortress. Though I had no idea what the stone was for, I kept it close to me, just because it had been something Wyatt had given me.

But here it was, a drawing of the stone staring back at me on the pages of this book.

This stone was called the Frost Pendant and it gave the wearer exceptional frost powers that could overpower almost any other type of magic.

I dropped the book on the floor and held on to the pendant. Closing my eyes, I invoked my powers and an avalanche rushed into my veins, making me gasp. Whoa, this pendant wasn't a trick.

I opened my eyes and stared at the bracelet around my wrist. I touched the pendant to it and willed it open.

The bracelet snapped with a loud crack and fell to the ground.

I stared at it in shock. Holy shit, it had worked! The bracelet was gone! I was free!

Which meant, I could escape. I could leave this place.

I picked up the bracelet and stuffed it into my pocket. I put the books back into their places, except for two fiction ones, and headed to the entrance. Somehow, I would trick the guards on our way back to my chambers, and I would make a run for it.

"Your highness," Jennie said with a bow of her head as she entered the library. "May I escort you back to your chambers?"

My brow furrowed. This wasn't how my plan was supposed to go, but I could work with this. "Yes."

On the way along the hallways, Jennie stayed a step behind me, while the guards followed us a few feet back.

Once we were back into my chambers and the doors were closed, I turned to Jennie.

"Have you ever wished you could escape this place?" I asked, knowing I was treading into dangerous waters.

"It's foolish to wish we could escape, your highness."

"But if you could," I insisted.

She paused, her eyes growing sorrowful. "Yes, if I could, I would escape this place."

My heart squeezed with hope. I could wait for a few more minutes or hours to escape if that meant I could take her with me. "Then, go to your room and pack a small bag. Tomorrow early morning, before the sun rises, meet me back here."

She stared at me, lost. "Why, your highness?"

"I'm going to make your wish come true."

20

As expected, the explosion caused confusion and most of the shadow fae guards went to check out what happened.

And I ran toward the prison. Holding the enchanted stone by the piece of cloth, I pressed it against one of the thick metal bars. It turned orange in a few seconds and quickly melted away. I repeated the action with at least other three bars, making a big hole for us to escape through.

Then I stepped into the prison. A remaining guard advanced on me. I sidestepped him, swiped his spear from him, and pierced his chest with it. I dropped the spear, and his body fell to the ground.

"Wyatt," someone called me. I looked at the voice. Holding on to bars, Daleigh stared at me. "What are you doing here?"

"Saving your ass." I didn't waste time. I pressed the stone on the lock of the cage's door, melting it in three seconds. I swung the door open. "Let's go before the guards come back this way."

"What about the others?" he asked, walking to my side. He was as tall as I was, but he had clearly lost weight in these past few weeks.

"I'll take care of it." I showed him the stone in my hand.

"I'm coming with you."

Not in the mood to argue, I directed the frost fae toward the hole that led out of the cages, then shuffled deeper into the prison camp. I melted another lock without any hitches and sent the fae in the same direction. When they hesitated, Daleigh told them it was all right, and they complied with him.

Great. I was the one doing the fucking rescue, and he would be the one to get a medal for it. I shook my head and pushed those thoughts away. I could be angry with him because he sold his sister to an evil prince, but now was not the time to argue about that.

First, I would save him. Then I would beat the crap out of him.

We reached the third and last cage. I pressed the stone on the lock and melted it.

"Stop!" someone shouted.

Daleigh turned to the new voice and I pulled the door open. "Go!" I told the fae, before turning to face the five guards who were pointing their spears at us. I handed the cloth wrapped stone to Daleigh. "Hold on to this."

Then I shifted into my wolf form.

I pounced into one of the guards, while Daleigh, too weakened, shot a ray of ice into another. I killed the first one too fast and turned to another. Just then, Ariella and Kayden joined us. The fallen angel and blaze fae used their magic and in less than a minute, we had killed the five fae guards.

We heard the shouts of more guards coming.

"Let's get out of here," Ariella said. She wrapped an arm around Daleigh's waist and helped him as we ran out of the prison.

WITHOUT ANOTHER PLACE TO GATHER, WE ENDED UP AT Farrah's and Daleigh's family manor. We knew we couldn't stay here for too long, but it was a good location to rest for a couple of hours and get organized.

After tending for the wounded, and feeding the weak, I called Daleigh to the back porch of the house, where no one would interrupt us.

Still weak, Daleigh leaned against the cold ice wall. "How did you find out about us?"

"Farrah did," I told him. Even with my werewolf blood, the air here was too cold for me. I crossed my arms, trying to remain warm. "She overhead some of Lark's advisors talking about what happened to you."

Daleigh frowned. "You talked to her? Where is she?"

"Still locked in the fortress. Lark put a bracelet on her wrist that doesn't allow her to leave the grounds. If she does, she'll die."

Daleigh cursed under his breath. "What have I done?"

I nodded as the anger I felt toward him came back full

throttle. "What have you done. Good question. As much as I would love to fucking punch you right now, we don't have time to lose. We need to rescue Farrah somehow. She said you would know what to do."

He shrugged. "The only thing I can think of is to gather as much of us we can, the ones who can still lift their weapons, and attack the Shade Fortress."

As much of us we can ... that sparked something in my mind. I inhaled deeply. "I have an idea."

21

FARRAH

As soon as Jennie left my chambers, I went around my room and grabbed a few things I might need and shoved them all inside a small bag. Thankfully, there wasn't much I wanted from this place.

I glanced at the cat, still lying on the armchair as if life was perfect. Well, for him it probably was. I frowned, wondering what I should do with it. Leave it? Hope he followed me? Scoop him up?

Not sure what to do about him, I went to bed and tried to sleep. I barely slept a wink but willed my body to rest. I would need it.

Around five in the morning, I gave up trying to rest and got ready.

The young fae said she would be back very early morning, but soon the sun would start rising and she wasn't here.

Then one hour passed. The sunlight was visible from behind the mountain.

Two hours. The sun was peeking above the trees.

I was starting to think something had happened. What if she was caught trying to pack? Trying to sneak in here with her bag? What if the poisoning investigation went south and they asked to interrogate her again, detaining her for longer?

Though I had never said it out loud, by now I believed she had to know I had been the one who tried to poison the prince. If they detained her, would she tell them what she knew?

Another hour passed.

In the end, I decided to wait all day, since it would be foolish to escape during the day, when it would be hard to hide. But once the sun started its descent, I was done. Jennie hadn't shown up the entire day, not even to bring me lunch, which was delivered by one of the guards. She either had been caught or had lost her nerve. Either way, she wouldn't be escaping with me.

I scooped the cat in my arms, inhaled a deep breath, and opened the doors to my chambers.

One of the guards turned to me. "May I help you, princess?" he asked. His words might be polite, but his tone was clipped, as if he detested talking to me.

"Yes." I opened my door wider. "All of you, look at this."

The other three guards turned to me.

With the Frost Pendant in my hand, I called on my magic. The immense rush flooded my veins, taking me by surprise. I wasn't used to this much magic at once.

"Princ—"

The guard's words died on his lips as I shot my magic

onto them. The four guards became ice sculptures. Using my powers, I pushed them inside my chambers and hid them inside my bathroom. Then I frosted over the bathroom's lock. By the time they thawed and were able to break through this door, I would be far, far gone.

Slipping through the fortress was easy with the Frost Pendant. I tried not engaging with anyone, but now my powers were so great, it was easy to trick them all. My only other challenge was the guards at the outer gates. Those I had to freeze too. I hid them inside the nearest room and once more frosted over the lock.

Then I raced out of the fortress and the cat jumped off my arms, running ahead of me. I inhaled the fresh air of the evening. The sun had already disappeared behind the mountain, giving me cover.

It gave them cover too.

I didn't see them emerging from the shadows until they were only a few steps in front of me. Soldiers. A lot of Shadow Fae soldiers, and all of them standing between my freedom and me.

This time, I wouldn't just bow my head and let them take me. This time, I had the Frost Pendant. This time, I would win.

I shot my hand out before any of them could react. The became frozen statues. I made my way through them.

"Your highness."

I whipped around and saw Jennie running to me. She had a small bag across her shoulders and big eyes.

"You came," I whispered as she stopped in front of me.

She offered me a small smile. "I was afraid I wouldn't be able to catch up."

I reached up and rested my hand on her shoulder. "You're here now. Let's go."

Jennie put her hand over mine. "I'm sorry," she said, her eyes glinting in the darkness. Quicker than I could blink, Jennie grabbed the Frost Pendant from my other hand.

I gaped at her. "Jennie!" I lunged at her.

But she retreated. Meanwhile, the soldiers thawed and surrounded me. I stared at Jennie, my eyes wild. "What have you done?"

She stepped out of the soldier's circle just as a new form took shape from the shadows.

Prince Lark.

He stood beside Jennie and extended her hand to her. She dropped the pendant on his hand, then lowered her head.

"Good girl," the prince said, his eyes on mine.

I clenched my fists. "Why would you betray me?" I asked Jennie. "He's despicable and I was going to help you escape."

Jennie kept her head lowered. "The prince promised not only freedom, but the means to live well."

He offered her money? That was why she betrayed me? I couldn't believe it.

The prince nodded. "You know, my faithful servant." He stepped back until he was looming over her. "I'm very good at lying." A shiny blade appeared in his hand and he slashed her throat.

I gasped, my hand over my mouth. Horror filled me.

Lark stepped over Jennie's body and approached me. "My dear Farrah. The Moon Period is over." He snapped his fingers to the soldiers. "Bring her to my chambers."

The soldiers reached for me.

I called on my magic and tried to freeze them again, but they were too many for me. When I froze one, another one showed up. I created an ice shield in between them and me.

Then the ice shattered.

"Enough games, Farrah," the prince snarled. He had broken the ice.

The soldiers clasped their heavy hands around my arms and they dragged me back inside the fortress.

22

WYATT

WE DIDN'T GO BACK TO THE HOUSE WE HAD BORROWED before. Instead, we went to Starlight Vale. I had sent a message to Luana and Keeran and they were waiting for us when we arrived.

Even before seeing Luana and Keeran, Romulus and Meira, Luana's right and left hands, met us at the entrance. Meira guided the injured to the infirmary and the others to a temporary housing, while Romulus took Daleigh, Ariella, Kayden and I to the main building at the town's center.

I glanced around as we walked through the paths forming roads—to the gray stone buildings, the brown tree branches entwining along the walls, the green leaves forming natural canopies. It was a beautiful, comforting town. But most impressive was the residents. Luana was the alpha of the Starlight pack, and Keeran was the Warlock Lord, and Starlight Vale was the home of magical werewolves and powerful warlocks.

Luana had invited me to stay here with them over three years ago, but I wasn't magical like her and her pack. I was a normal werewolf. Despite her good intentions, I had never belonged here. That was why I left.

We approached the main building, which looked like a tall castle in the middle of town, and my steps faltered. Luana and Keeran stood atop the stairs at the front door, waiting for us.

For me.

When Luana saw me, she pressed a hand to her mouth.

I stopped a few feet from them. "Hey," I said, suddenly feeling very lame. I had been a teenager when I had last seen them, and for many years, Luana had been my idol. In a way, I knew she had always considered me a kid, maybe even her kid, her responsibility. But in these three years, I had grown. I had matured. The demons still lived inside my head, sure, but I had a better handle on them now.

Suddenly serious, Luana growled and lunged at me. She punched my shoulder hard. "You pest!" She fixed her hazel eyes in mine. "You left without saying goodbye. I was so damn worried." Then she flung her arms around my neck. "It's so good to see you," she whispered.

Stunned, it took me a second to act. But then I hugged her too. It felt different now. I was taller, wider, and she was smaller in my arms. "I missed you too."

Luana pulled back and patted my cheek. "Pull another prank like that and I'll skin you alive."

I chuckled. "I'll keep that in mind."

Keeran walked up to us, a small smile on his lips. "Welcome back, Wyatt." He clasped my hand firmly. "Come inside. Let's get comfortable so we can talk."

Luana and Keeran guided us to a large seating room. Aspen and Boise, Keeran's warlocks, had set up the room with drinks and lots of food. Since I was in much need of a break, I grabbed a bottle of beer and tipped it over, chugging it fast.

Luana raised an eyebrow at me. "Are you okay?"

I let out a heavy sigh. "I will be when all of this is over."

Her hazel eyes narrowed. "Tell me what's going on."

So I did. I reminded them about Farrah's deal with the evil shadow fae prince, and then I told them the rest: finding Farrah again, running from the prince, the prince's promise to let her people go back to the fae realm, imprisoning Farrah with that fucking bracelet, his lies and locking her people in a prison camp, and us breaking them out.

Though, I didn't tell them about my deal with Drollmor, or that the Bonecrown witches were around, looking for Farrah.

I stared at Luana, hoping she still had some kind of affection for me. "We were able to rally six other frost fae who aren't too weak or hurt to help us, but that's not enough."

"You want our help," Keeran said, his tone flat.

I swallowed, suddenly nervous. "Yes."

Like true mates, Luana and Keeran exchanged a look. An entire conversation passed through their eyes in matters of seconds.

Finally, Luana glanced at me again. A slow smile crept up her lips. "Of course we'll help you."

It took over a day to organize everything, get werewolves and warlocks together, and move out to the Shade Fortress. An entire fucking day Farrah remained in that place, suffering at the hands of that crazy prince.

But once we arrived, it didn't take long to put our plan in action.

As soon as the sun went down behind the mountain, Luana and Keeran led an army of a hundred wolves and warlocks, marching directly to the fortress front doors. They launched an assault the moment they were in close range, sending bolts of magic and ripping the throat of the fae who dared try to defend the fortress.

While they kept the soldiers busy and snatched the attention of the shadow prison, Ariella, Kayden, Daleigh, and I sneaked through the back. This time, we didn't bother putting on glamours. We attacked the soldiers guarding the back gates full on.

With the surprise, they went down easily.

And then we entered the fortress.

23

FARRAH

I wasn't taken directly to Prince Lark's chambers, as I thought. First, I was taken to my own bedroom, where I was ordered to bathe, then change into my most beautiful gown. A young female fae came in when I was getting dressed, to help me with my makeup and my hair. The poor thing didn't look up once, and her hands shook so hard ...

I couldn't blame her. By now the entire fortress must have heard I tried escaping and that Jennie died in the process.

My stomach contracted. The other female fae, the winemaker, and now Jennie. All of them had died at the ends of the fae prince—because of me. Their deaths were on me, and I would never forgive myself for that.

After I was all dolled up, the guards guided me to Lark's chambers on the other side of the fortress. They pushed me inside and closed the doors behind me with a definite thud.

I was locked in here with the evil prince.

Dressed in his best suit, Lark turned to me with a wide smile. "You look beautiful." I winced. Coming from him, this compliment meant nothing. He stalked to me, like a predator sizing up his prey. "Relax, my dear Farrah. I'm not mad at you. I'm actually very amused and impressed. You have skills. You're a strong fae, which means our children will be stronger than both of us together."

I winced again, but this time I held on to the disgust that rolled within me. "We'll never have children."

Lark halted just a foot in front of me. "Of course we will. And we'll start working on it tonight." He gestured to his large bed across the room.

I shook my head, my eyes never leaving his. "You don't understand. I can't have your children, because I've already been with someone else."

His dark eyes widened and his breathing stopped. A sheen of rage changed his expression from amusement to fury. He balled his hands. "You're lying. You're stalling so I won't take you to my bed."

"Here." I showed him the looking glass I had brought with me. "See it for yourself."

The prince's brows curled down. Hesitant, he picked up the looking glass. He paced in front of me, his eyes glued to the looking glass as the images showed him the truth. I didn't try seeing what he was seeing. I knew that somehow the looking glass would show him about Wyatt and me.

About my mate.

With a roar, Lark threw the looking glass on the dark

stone floor, shattering it in a million pieces. I flinched from the flying shards but held my ground. I wouldn't succumb to fear now.

With murderous eyes, Lark lunged at me. He closed his hand around my neck. "If you can't be really mine, then you won't be anyone's." Dark shadows appeared around him. His magic. "I'll hurt you, I'll torture you, and then I'll kill you."

I gasped, even though I knew this was coming.

He tightened his grip and I gagged. *Focus, Farrah.* I clutched his shirt and tugged him even closer. As fast as I could, I slipped my hands on his pants pockets. Bingo. My right hand closed around the Frost Pendant.

Instantly, my powers came alive and I embraced them.

Lark's eyes rounded as he noticed what I had done. His grip loosened around my neck. With a wicked smile of my own, I rested my hands over his chest and sent my magic into him.

Inch by inch, the frost spread over his skin, inside his body, around his organs. In less than a minute, Lark had become a frozen statue.

I let out a long breath.

This wasn't over yet.

Grunting, I pushed Lark's frozen form until it tipped over and fell on the floor. He shattered just like the looking glass had. A million pieces scattered on the dark floor.

Prince Lark was dead.

I didn't waste time. I flung the doors of his chambers open and ran out. The guards turned to me, but before they could blink, I had frozen them too.

I ran through the hallway and down the stairs. That was when I realized something was wrong. The only other guards I had seen were running to the front of the fortress.

Then a muted boom shook the fortress.

We were under attack?

"Farrah!"

I turned around, my hands up to send my magic out. But my shoulders sagged in relief. It was Wyatt, and behind him were Daleigh, Ariella, and a blaze fae. A blaze fae? I shook my head, not caring about that right now.

"You've come," I said.

Wyatt grabbed my hand, holding tight. His eyes landed on my wrist, bracelet-free. A small smile crept up his lips. "Let's get out of here."

24

It was easier to sneak into the fortress, and then out, since it was in chaos because of Luana's and Keeran's attack. While we ran out, we had to fight only a handful of soldiers.

Once we exited through the back, Farrah told us about the Frost Pendant, how she got rid of the bracelet, and about killing the fae prince. I almost tripped at my own feet when she said that. Not that I was shocked she did, but then because our mission here was done. All we had to do now was make his soldiers surrender so we could take over the Shade Fortress, and Kayden could claim it.

But as we made our way to the front of the fortress to join Luana's and Keeran's forces, the ground began shaking.

Suddenly, dark smoke rose from the ground near the fortress, black and thick.

Magical.

We ran faster, putting some distance between us and the fortress as the smoke rose up and up, covering the fortress in darkness.

We reached the front of the fortress, where the battle seemed to have paused as fae, werewolves, and warlocks gaped at the thick smoke rising to the sky.

The ground shook again, stronger this time.

In the middle of the fray, Luana shifted back into her human form and yelled. "Pull back!"

The Starlight werewolves and the warlocks didn't waste time. They followed her orders. And it wasn't a fucking minute late as the ground trembled again and broke, opening up between us and the fortress.

"Run!" Keeran shouted.

I held on to Farrah's hand tighter and we ran with the others, away from the fortress and whatever was happening to it.

When I glanced over my shoulder, I didn't see any shadow fae anymore. Had they been swallowed by the pit, or consumed by the smoke, or had they made it back inside?

After running for a few minutes, we stopped at the top of a hill, a safe distance from the fortress. Though it wasn't a fortress anymore. The shadows slowly dissipated into the air and what appeared was a tall black castle, with long spires and thick stone walls.

And right on top of the wide balcony on the tallest middle tower, was a terrifying figure.

The Fae King.

He didn't say a single word—not that we would be able

to hear him from here, unless he used some kind of magic. No, he simply raised his hands and the world shuddered with an electric current.

The pit around the new castle filled with black water and from the castle emerged dark soldiers. They formed a circle around the new mote, their long spears at ready should we attack again.

"What do we do now?" Ariella asked from behind me.

Farrah's shoulders sagged. "I know what he wants. He wants revenge for his son." She turned wide, blue eyes at me. "He wants me."

I shook my head. "What? And you're thinking about going to him?"

"If it's the only way to stop him ..."

"Don't be stupid." That was Keeran. He stepped closer and Farrah stared in shock at him and Luana. "We won't let you walk to your death."

"Besides," Luana started. "We know his type. Even if you sacrifice yourself, he won't stop now. You know that."

I squeezed Farrah's hand. "Let's just take a break, even a short one. We can come up with a plan to defeat him later."

"Wyatt is right," Luana said. "We can talk about this king after we are all rested and tended for." She gestured to her people, to the frost fae, and to my friends. "Let's go back to Starlight Vale."

Without waiting for a reply, she turned and marched deeper into the woods. Keeran was right at her heels. The werewolves and the warlocks were next. Then the frost fae.

Daleigh paused, but followed, along with Ariella and Kayden.

I tugged on Farrah's hand. "Come on."

She resisted for a second, but let me guide her to safety.

25

ON THE WAY TO STARLIGHT VALE, I SAW SOMETHING NO ONE else did: a magical image on the night sky of a bone and a crown. It wasn't the symbol of the Bonecrown witches, but I understood the meaning.

Once we made it to the beautiful city, Romulos and Meira took us to the guests' quarter, where accommodations had already been set up earlier. Apparently, after rescuing Daleigh and the frost fae, Wyatt, Ariella, and Kayden, the blaze fae, had come here asked for Keeran's and Luana's help.

"You have to tell her," Ariella said, looking pointedly at Wyatt right at the door of Wyatt's assigned bedroom. She briefly shifted her gaze to me, then disappeared into her own bedroom.

I frowned. "What was that about?"

Wyatt groaned. He opened the door and gestured for me to get in. Once we were inside, he closed the door and faced me. "I promised her I would tell you something after we rescued you."

My frown deepened. "Tell me what?"

Wyatt crossed his arms. "You first. What do the Bonecrown witches want with you?"

That got me by surprise. "How do you know that?"

"Because I ran into them. Now tell me."

I let out a long sigh. "When we were first banished into the human realm, we ended up unknowingly creating a camp into Bonecrown territory. First, they scared us to death. Later they chased us away. However, they didn't stop attacking and harassing us." I started pacing, the beat of my heart speeding. "After some battles, they offered a solution. If we gave them a powerful fae as a sacrifice, they would call it quits. They would let us go."

Wyatt inhaled sharply. "You were that fae."

I halted. "It was a random drawing, but yes, I was selected."

Wyatt shook his head. "But ... when we rescued you. Luana, and I ... you were tied up because of the Bonecrowns. Why hadn't they killed you yet?"

"They were going to. They left me there to inflict pain and fear into me. They would come back the next day to finish me off."

"But we rescued you first."

I nodded, ashamed I had never told them—him—the truth before. "I didn't want to die." I let out a long breath. "I heard they went after Daleigh and the others, but none of them had their magic as strong as mine. The Bonecrown didn't settle. They looked for me."

Wasn't it ironic? I had escaped from being a sacrifice to the witches, just to end up as a sacrifice of sorts to Prince Lark. Either way, I had been sold to save my people —twice.

And even that I couldn't do right, since Lark had lied about letting my people go.

"What happened then?"

I shrugged. "They must have found me again after I married Lark? That's the only thing I can think of."

"So what now? We'll have to add them to our list of evil beings to face?"

A hollow chuckle escaped past my lips, but it died a second after. "What about you? What Ariella was referring to?"

He ran a heavy hand over his thick hair and hesitated. "A while back, I sold my soul to a higher demon, Drollmor."

I stared at him, incredulous. "You did what? Why the hell would you sell your soul?"

"For a chance to see you again," he whispered.

My heart cracked a little. I couldn't deny it. Since the moment we first met, I knew Wyatt and I were connected, that we shared a destiny. Then we found out we were mates.

He had sold his soul to find me again.

How could I be mad at that? I would probably have done the same thing.

Though, a small flicker of fury started in me. How was he so stupid? The demon would never rest until he got Wyatt's soul!

His hazel eyes held such an intense and scared shine, my heart cracked some more. Without a word, I went to him and wrapped my arms around his wide shoulders.

"We'll fix this," I promised, whispering in his ear. "We'll figure out how to defeat the Bonecrowns, this higher demon, and the Fae King."

His hands splayed on the small of my back. "I believe you."

When he lowered his head to mine, I met him halfway. His lips landed on mine and I let out a sigh. He was mine and I was his, and I just wanted to enjoy that for a moment.

His kiss started soft, slow, as if he wanted to make sure I wouldn't run away this time. I wouldn't, so I grabbed his shoulders hard and deepened the kiss. Wyatt let out a groan and scooped me up. Without breaking the kiss, he took me to the bed.

This time, when we made love, we didn't hold back. The mating bond screamed at us, making everything we felt stronger, more powerful. Every millisecond, I thought I would burst into a million pieces of pure pleasure.

Nothing could be better than being on Wyatt's arms.

It wasn't the first time I slipped from Wyatt's bed, but it would be the last.

Careful not to wake him, I got dressed and after a long look at his peaceful, sleeping form, I sneaked out of the bedroom.

I didn't encounter anyone around the guests' quarter, though I almost bumped into two warlocks patrolling the streets of Starlight Vale. Using my powers enhanced by the Frost Pendant, I scaled the side of a building and hid on the roof.

Then I skipped from roof to roof, until I was outside the city's limits.

I dared to peek at the beautiful city one last time. I was proud of what Keeran and Luana had done here. They were really a great pair and they people should see only happiness.

Which meant, I had to deal with the Bonecrown and the Fae King by myself, without involving no one else. I was tired of seeing my friends suffering, or being used against me.

It would be only me now.

Pulling the hood of my cloak over my head, I took in a long breath and gave the first step toward my new mission.

———

Continue reading about Wyatt and Farrah on *The Blood Pact*!

THANK YOU

Thank you for reading *The Fae Bound*!

Reviews are very important for authors. If you liked my book, please consider leaving a review on your favorite online retailer and/or on goodreads!

You can grab the next book on the series now:

The Blood Pact

Don't forget to sign up for my Newsletter to find out about new releases, cover reveals, giveaways, and more!

If you want to see exclusive teasers, help me decide on covers, read excerpts, talk about books, etc, join my reader group on Facebook: Juliana's Club!

ABOUT THE AUTHOR

While USA Today Bestselling Author Juliana Haygert dreams of being Wonder Woman, Buffy, or a blood elf shadow priest, she settles for the less exciting—but equally gratifying—life as a wife, a mother, and an author. She resides in North Carolina and spends her days writing about kick-ass heroines and the heroes who drive them crazy.

Subscribe to her mailing list to receive emails of announcement, events, and other fun stuff related to her writing and her books: www.bit.ly/JuHNL

For more information:
www.julianahaygert.com

facebook.com/julianahaygert

twitter.com/juliana_haygert

instagram.com/juliana.haygert

goodreads.com/juliana_haygert

pinterest.com/julianahaygert

bookbub.com/authors/juliana-haygert

ALSO BY JULIANA HAYGERT

To find links and more info, go to:

www.julianahaygert.com/books/

Shorts

Into the Darkest Fire

Tested

Rite World: Blackthorn Hunters Academy

The Demon Kiss (Book 1)

The Hunter Secret (Book 2)

The Soul Bond (Book 3)

The Shadow Trials (Book 4)

The Infernal Curse (Book 5)

Rite World

The Vampire Heir (Book 1)

The Witch Queen (Book 2)

The Immortal Vow (Book 3)

The Warlock Lord (Book 4)

The Wolf Consort (Book 5)

The Crystal Rose (Book 6)

The Wolf Forsaken (Book 7)

The Fae Bound (Book 8)

The Blood Pact (Book 9)

The Wyth Courts

Winter King (Book 1)

Spring Warrior (Book 2)

Summer Prince (Book 3)

Autumn Rebel (Book 4)

The Fire Heart Chronicles

Heart Seeker (Book 1)

Flame Caster (Book 2)

Sorrow Bringer (Book 3)

Earth Shaker (Novella)

Soul Wanderer (Book 4)

Fate Summoner (Book 5)

War Maiden (Book 6)

The Everlast Series

Destiny Gift (Book 1)

Soul Oath (Book 2)

Cup of Life (Book 3)

Everlasting Circle (Book 4)

Willow Harbor Series

Hunter's Revenge (Book 3)

Siren's Song (Book 5)

Breaking Series

Breaking Free (Book 1)

Breaking Away (Book 2)

Breaking Through (Book 3)

Breaking Down (Book 4)

Standalones

Daughter of Darkness